A Christmas
To Remember

By
Pam Pottorff

"Christmas is a season not only of rejoicing but of reflection.

-Winston Churchill

Any resemblance to persons living or dead should be plainly apparent to them and those who know them. The events written in this book actually happened, although the author has taken small liberties due to her failing memory over the years.

First paperback edition 2021

Book cover design by Pam Pottorff
Photographs by Pam Pottorff

This book is dedicated to my huge, wild and wacky family. Without all of you, my life would be boring.

Preface

I have been a Christmas fanatic from the day I was born. Okay, that may be a slight exaggeration, but certainly my fascination with the holiday began at a very early age. I have always loved the sights, sounds, and spirit of the season, but it wasn't until I read this quote from Winston Churchill that I began to reflect on my Christmas experiences with more depth. "Christmas is a season not only of rejoicing but of reflection," Churchill wrote. This was a call to action for me not only to write down my Christmas memories, but also to reflect on the events leading to these experiences. In the end, I found these reflections not only to be insightful but life changing. It is my hope that this book will be your call to action to reflect on your Christmas memories. Perhaps, you too, will find insight leading a deeper appreciation of life.

A Christmas to Remember

Table of Contents

Faith Versus Fantasy

"Faith carries the light of truth which eliminates the shadow of doubt."

-Author Unknown

Being able to distinguish reality from fantasy is a milestone in human development. For me, this began happening at my eighth Christmas.

My three older sisters and older brother had all married and left home to start new lives. My six-year-old brother, Kevin, and I were left at home with our parents. The hustle and bustle of having the older kids around was gone. Suddenly, our home seemed quiet and slightly lonely.

Even putting up the Christmas tree that year seemed very uneventful. One Saturday afternoon in December, Dad hauled the box containing our Christmas tree down from the upstairs bedroom. Mom, Kevin, and I carried the smaller boxes containing the lights, ornaments, and garland. Once we placed the boxes in a pile in the dining room, Dad and Kevin magically disappeared leaving Mom and me with the task of decorating our home for the holidays.

Many people venture to nearby forests to cut their own Christmas trees but not my family. We lived on the plains of North Central Iowa. While our farm was located on the shores of Iowa Lake and was surrounded by a wooded area, all of the

9

trees were deciduous such as elms, oaks, and maples. Live evergreen trees were a prime commodity in our neck of the woods, so we solved the problem by having an artificial tree. Ours was not just any artificial tree. It was made of aluminum foil, which was very stylish in the late sixties.

The tree assembly began with Mom putting a wooden pole, which was about the height and diameter of a broomstick in a metal stand. My job was to remove each "branch" from the brown paper tube protecting it. Once released from the paper tube, the foil foliage of each branch seemed to explode, including the circular flower shape at the end of each limb. I handed these fluffy, metal masterpieces to Mom, beginning with the longest branches first, and she meticulously placed them in the correct holes drilled into the wooden pole. The triangular shape of the tree soon was complete, and the aluminum fringe sparkled in the fluorescent lighting of the dining room chandelier.

Rather than a string of lights, we had a single floodlight situated next to the tree so it could shine on the metallic boughs. Red and green glass bulbs on the branches completed the tree. Each bulb reminded me of a miniature funhouse mirror, and I enjoyed seeing the distorted image of my face in the reflection on every bulb. I made my own fun by sticking out my tongue and crossing my eyes to add to the goofiness.

Since it was too fragile for me to handle, Mom removed the ancient nativity scene from a box and placed it under the tree. The small ragged cardboard barn was held together with scotch tape that was yellow from age and crispy to the touch. The people and animals, which inhabited the cardboard stable, were made of genuine plastic. The painted details of each piece had chipped off over the years, creating the illusion that each small statue was an artifact from an archeological dig. Miraculously, the only piece that had escaped any damage was the angel, which hung at the peak of the tiny building. Even though this nativity scene was old and tattered, my mother would never replace it with a new one because it was an important part of our family's Christmas traditions.

After the tree was complete, we decorated the rest of our home with holiday candles, felt elves, Santa figurines, sprigs of plastic holly, and evergreen garland adorned with red, velvet bows. When the storage boxes were empty, Mom and I toted them back to the spare bedroom.

That evening, Mom conjured a delicious home cooked meal while I set the table. Dad and Kevin came in from feeding the livestock and joined us for the evening meal. When the food was gone, the dishes were washed and dried, and the kitchen was clean, we all retired to the living room to enjoy our favorite television shows.

Mom was engulfed in her brown velvet chair that rocked and swiveled. Dad was at ease in his green recliner with the footrest popped out and the back tilted toward the wall. Kevin and I took our assigned seats on the carpet in front of the television. We watched "The Lawrence Welk Show" in all of its black and white glory until it was bath time.

Our old farmhouse had only one bathroom on the main floor next to my parents' bedroom. Mother ran a tub of hot water in which she quickly bathed and scrubbed Kevin. Once he had his pajamas on, Mom set him free, and it was my turn. I always took my bath last. Mother insisted that I use the same tub of water my brother had used, which was cold and cloudy with soap scum. Needless to say, I bathed quickly every Saturday night, which was the only night we took a bath. Shivering, I put on my flannel nightgown and threw my dirty clothes down the clothes shoot to land in a basket in the basement. Mom joined me in the bathroom to roll my hair in pink sponge curlers. Soon Kevin and I were climbing the steep stairs to the second floor of the farmhouse where our bedrooms were located.

The entire second floor of our home was heated by one vent located on the floor in the hallway at the top of the stairs. As a child, I remember the furnace never seemed to turn off during the winter although I am sure it did. Even though it seemed like hot air came through the floor vent continuously, the bedrooms upstairs were always cold. Our remedy to this problem was to stand on the floor vent, which made our pajamas puff up like hot air balloons, making us laugh and giggle uncontrollably. We stood on the vent until we could no longer endure the hot metal and the designs of the grate were pressed into the soles of our feet. Then we would run to our bedrooms and slip between the frigid sheets. We'd yell to Dad that we were in bed, and he would shut off the hall light with the switch at the bottom of the stairs.

Usually, I fell asleep immediately but not on this particular night. Visions of Mom and me assembling the tree and decorating the house floated through my mind as well as lessons from our religious education classes on Wednesday nights. We were learning about Mary, Joseph, and baby Jesus and how they became a family. We learned that Jesus was God's son, and God the Father sent Jesus to earth so that we could all go to heaven. That was a lot for an eight-year-old mind to ponder. No wonder I couldn't sleep.

I slipped out of bed into the chilly air in my room and made my way to the hall. I was tempted to step briefly on the floor vent to warm myself, but I was on a mission so I passed it by and continued down the stairs.

Mother had left the floodlight on the silver Christmas tree as a nightlight in case one of us had to come downstairs to use the bathroom during the night. As I sat cross-legged in front of the rickety manger scene, I began picking up each person and animal statue. The Christmas story we had learned in catechism class kept replaying in my head. What was real here? Was it the Christmas story? Was it Christ's birth? I looked around the room at the other decorations. What about Santa Claus and the elves that helped him? What about flying reindeer and talking snowmen? What did holly berries, mistletoe, and bells that jingled have to do with Christ's birth? It all seemed very disconnected. I was so confused. What was real and what was not real? At that moment, I couldn't tell so I closed my eyes, folded my hands in prayer, and asked God what was the true meaning of Christmas.

God's answer came to me in a vision.
I could see the young virgin Mary holding her newborn child close to her chest, the child being comforted by the sound of His mother's beating heart. Mary being comforted by the warmth of her child's body against hers, and Joseph looking on the scene contemplating his new role as father and protector. I felt a wonderful tingling feeling spread throughout my entire body. I opened my eyes and realized I had found the true meaning of Christmas while sitting at the base of the artificial Christmas tree made of aluminum foil, holding a plastic baby Jesus. The real meaning of Christmas had nothing to do with Santa Claus, reindeer, elves, or talking snowmen.

"Thank you, God," I whispered as I kissed baby Jesus and placed Him back in the small cardboard barn beside his loving parents.

I journeyed back up the stairs, stopping to warm myself on the heat vent. The hot air instantly puffed up my nightgown, and soon my feet felt like they were on fire. I ran into my room and slipped between the frosty sheets. I had relied on my faith rather than believing in fantasy. I fell asleep with a contented smile on my face because under the artificial tree, I found the real reason for Christmas. . . the birth of Jesus.

Reflections

•Never forget the real meaning of Christmas is the celebration of the miracle of Christ's birth.

•God gives us exactly what we need just when we need it, whether it is the words in a daily devotional, the message in a sermon seemly written just for you, a song filled with special meaning sung at Sunday service, the answer to a child's question about the real meaning of Christmas, or the birth of the Christ child to save our souls.

•God's love is like the hallway heat vent. It is always on, and we know just where to find it. You can stand on it as long as you want basking in the warmth and love before venturing out into the cold world. Once you venture out into reality, you can always return to warm and recharge yourself.

Pam, Kevin(brother),Robb (nephew),
and the aluminum tree

The Driveway and
The Christmas Lights

"We are not human beings on a spiritual journey.
We are spiritual beings on a human journey."
                                        -Stephen Covey

"Kevin won again!" a small first grader screeched as my younger brother hopped up the steps of the big, yellow school bus that had pulled into our driveway. By the time I reached the bus, Kevin had claimed a seat in the "prime real estate" section at the back of the bus.

Our driveway led to my family's unique property in rural North Central Iowa close to the Minnesota border. The property included many fields of rich, black soil my father farmed, but it also included the shoreline of beautiful Iowa Lake. Mom utilized her entrepreneurial skills and her imagination, to create a lakeside resort where people could park their trailer homes, pitch tents, or rent rustic cabins. Boating and fishing were common recreational activities during the summer months. When fall arrived, many people would travel from Chicago to hunt deer and pheasants or to enjoy the peaceful scenery as the leaves changed from green to red, gold, and orange.

Part of the ambience of our rural resort for these city dwellers was the seclusion. The long driveway led to our big, white farmhouse, which could be seen from the highway, but the campsites and cabins were concealed in the woods behind our home. The only access to this hidden hideaway was the quaint, gravel driveway, which was about a half mile long.

"Don't you ever get tired of walking down that long driveway?" the other kids on the bus would ask. On the contrary, we never saw the gravel path in negative terms. We only saw the positives.

One positive aspect was it taught us to be resourceful. Living on the flat plains of Iowa allowed us to see the school bus several miles away. We would diligently sit on the counter by the kitchen sink in order to watch out of the window. When we spotted the bus on the eastern horizon, we would begin our journey down the driveway to meet the bus on time. This was an ingenious plan except for the days when we were messing around in the house instead of watching out of the window. A blast from the school bus horn would send us exploding from the house, sprinting down the driveway in a footrace that mirrored an Olympic track and field event. If you were a gambling person, you would have bet on my younger brother. He won the race down the driveway every time and was greeted first by the cheering bus riders and driver. Fortunately, I always came in a close second, which seemed logical since there were only two of us. A wonderful by-product of these sibling footraces was that my brother became a high school superstar in football, basketball, and track.

While the other kids saw our driveway as a curse, we viewed it as a gift. Not only was it a track for many footraces, it was also a raceway for our many modes of transportation, which symbolized our growth and journey towards adulthood.

Like many elementary-aged kids, we owned old, rickety, one-speed bicycles our mom had purchased for us at a local farm sale. At that point in our development, we let our imaginations run wild on a daily basis. We transformed those moving pieces of junk into super crazy "hot wheels." By using wooden clothespins, we simply attached playing cards to the front and back forks of the bike frames. Once we began pedaling, the playing cards flapped against the bike spokes creating a motor sound that roared through the quiet, country air. We would increase our horsepower by increasing the number of playing cards. At times we attached an entire deck of cards to our bikes. Our "motor" bikes sounded fantastic but looked like odd, abstract porcupines with a multitude of wooden clothespins protruding from the bike frames.

As we entered junior high, we outgrew our bikes physically and emotionally. We were ready to give up our playing card motors for something with real horsepower. Fortunately, Dad felt the same way in terms of our development with transportation, so he splurged and bought us a used go-cart. This was at a time in history when no one wore a seat belt when riding in a car. In fact, the majority of the time, we were fighting over who would get to lay in the back window of our family's car in order to fully enjoy the rays of the sun. So of course, we didn't wear a helmet when driving the go-cart. We didn't even own a helmet. We would simply let the wind blow through our hair with wild abandonment. The go-cart was nothing more than a glorified riding lawn mower, but to us it might as well have been an Indy racecar. Its speed and close proximity to the ground meant when you drove it, you returned covered in dust, with grit in your teeth, and a couple of bumps on your skull from a few small rocks that had jumped up from the road and hit you in the head. But we never cried or complained because we knew that would be the end of our beloved speed machine. A little bit of gravel in your shorts and a few lumps on the head were a small price to pay for all the fun we enjoyed.

As we entered high school, our tastes in recreational transportation became a little more refined, or that is what we liked to think. We were successful in converting Dad to our way of thinking as well, and we convinced him to trade in our old, dusty, rust covered go-cart for a shiny, new, red motorcycle. Instead of the line of dust the go-cart created as it zoomed down the driveway, the motorcycle with its shiny, red paint, and silvery chrome created the effect of a blazing orb traveling at the speed of light. We had come a long way from bikes, playing cards, and wooden clothespins.

While our modes of transportation may have changed over the years, the one thing that was constant was the Christmas lights, which adorned the outside of our rural home. Our old white farmhouse had two stories. The colorful Christmas lights lined the second story roof and the roof of the first story with its wrap around porch. As if that wasn't enough illumination, our father had constructed a huge five foot wooden star covered in lights and hung it on the second story between my bedroom window and my brother's bedroom window. Often the glare from the Christmas lights kept us up at night if they were not extinguished at a reasonable hour. Clearly, our home could have been the inspiration for the Griswold family's home illumination from the movie *Christmas Vacation.*

While having a well-lit home at Christmas is not unusual, leaving the lights up all year long year after year was a little on the strange side. Fortunately, there was a unique aspect to this phenomenon. Yes, there was actually logic behind the madness. There were times when we would not ride the bus because we were sick or our mom would take us to school usually because my brother had to return his tuba to the band room and that beautiful, behemoth piece of brass wasn't allowed on the bus. At those times,

Mom would simply flick the Christmas lights on and off as a signal to the bus driver to move on to the next stop. What a stroke of genius.

When the resort guests were trying to find our home in a rainstorm, blizzard, or on a late night trip from Chicago, the lights were similar to a lighthouse leading travelers to comfort and safety.

I didn't realize it until later in my life that our driveway and our permanent Christmas lights were a metaphor for life. The driveway represented the path of life. The modes of transportation represented the choices we make on how we travel on that path. The Christmas lights represented God's eternal light, always bright and ever present. We have the choice of traveling towards the light or away from it. Those lights led to our beautiful, peaceful resort, which represented heaven, the ultimate destination.

I learned from the driveway and those permanent Christmas lights, that when you change the way you look at things, the things you look at change. It is all a matter of perspective.

Reflections
•Life is about the choices we make. Do we travel away from God's light and the ultimate destination of heaven, or do we travel towards it?

• Life is an exquisite struggle to balance the changes (the different forms of transportation) with the constants (the driveway). It is through the necessary struggle between constants and changes that we learn, grow, and develop.

Our farm and resort on Iowa Lake

Guess Who is Coming to Christmas?

"In the giving-is the getting."

-David Matoc

Salt and pepper shakers, coins, books, and cats are just a few things that individuals normally collect. One of the many traits we all appreciated about my mother was she rarely did anything the "normal" way. Instead of collecting things, Mom collected people. She had a wonderful assortment of friends, but the people she liked to collect the most were those who were in need of a family. Since a family is a collection of people, she simply added these individuals to our family. None of us minded. In fact, we liked it. We loved watching our family grow with an assortment of people of all different shapes, sizes, colors, ages, and backgrounds.

When Aunt Margaret and her husband divorced, their children Terry and Gloria found a new home with us for a while because they needed a family. When Aunt Betty lost her battle with cancer, Uncle Red was left with the task of raising three small children. Soon, these cousins were at our house because they needed a family. Now, when I think about it, we needed them, too. Those wonderful kids taught us about strength and courage during life's most difficult times, and they were a welcomed distraction from our siblings.

Fortunately for many people, you didn't have to be a relative to be included in our family. The only qualification was that you had to be a human being. For many years, our family lived on a farm in North Central Iowa, but the property was distinctly different because it bordered Iowa Lake. Mother's entrepreneurial spirit led her to develop the lakeshore into a resort complete with campsites and rustic cabins. A few people left trailer homes on the lakeshore. These temporary structures became permanent summer homes. Of course, these summer residents immediately became adopted into our family. We spent hours hanging out at Grandpa and Grandma Smoker's trailer, eating snacks and watching them make crafts. Each summer evening, we would watch Grandpa Jorgenson clean fish on a stump by our house as he told us stories about his life as a younger man. Dean and Georgia Wilson often invited us to their summer dwelling to enjoy sweet treats, refreshing glasses of lemonade, and assorted candies that Mother would never let us eat. They were our version of the favorite aunt and uncle who spoil you when your parents aren't around, and they always referred to the treats as "our little secret." But whom were we kidding? Mother was no fool. She knew we were being fed contraband food.

Our family always seemed to increase its membership during Christmas. If there was a neighbor, relative, or friend who didn't have a place to celebrate the holidays, they knew they had an open invitation to our family's festivities.

Later in their lives, my parents moved from their large farmhouse into a home on the golf course in town. The only time my father voiced a concern about downsizing was at Christmas. He was concerned all the people Mom liked to invite wouldn't fit in our new home, so he asked her to "tone it down a little bit."

Interestingly enough, my mother lived life "loudly" with gusto and grit. She had no idea what "tone it down" meant so Dad spelled it out for her. She could invite anyone she wanted to our home before Christmas for coffee or club meetings, but on Christmas Day, the celebration was for our immediate family only, with one exception. My maternal grandmother, Grandma Mart, lived in the nursing home in our small town. Dad agreed when Mom went to pick up Grandma on Christmas morning, she could bring one carload of nursing home residents.

I could see the wheels turning in my mother's head as she tried to figure out how she could cram as many elderly people as she could into our gigantic, blue Chrysler. I had visions of our family car rolling through Main Street with people's heads, arms, and legs sticking out of the windows along with walkers, canes, and oxygen tank hoses.

For our first Christmas in our home in town, we went to midnight mass on Christmas Eve. When the sun rose on Christmas morning, so did we. We bustled around the house, each completing our assigned tasks to make the day a complete success.

Around eleven o'clock, Mom instructed me to put on my coat and boots because she and I were going to pick up Grandma and our mystery guests at the nursing home. I seemed to be the perfect candidate for this endeavor. I was a high school student, and I worked at the nursing home in the kitchen after school and in the laundry department on the weekends. The staff and residents were all my friends.

To be honest, Grandma Mart had delusions of being royalty. She thought she was a queen, and she expected to be treated as such. So of course, she was the first person we loaded into the car in the place of honor . . . the passenger seat.

"Who is next?" I questioned Mom as we headed back into the building. I knew she had a plan, but she hadn't shared it with me yet.

"Well, we've got to take Nettie. We just can't take Grandma and leave her roommate sitting there alone."

Nettie had been Grandma Mart's roommate for many years, yet we had never seen a member of her family, so naturally she became a member of our family. When we showed up at the doorway of the room, Nettie questioned, "Did you forget something?"

"No," Mom replied. "You're going with us."

I will never forget the look on sweet Nettie's face for as long as I live. It was as if she were Cinderella being whisked away to the ball in our huge, blue Chrysler instead of a pumpkin carriage. We quickly bundled up our friend in her wool coat, scarf, and gloves. As Mom helped Princess Nettie into the backseat, I folded her metal walker and laid it on top of Grandma's wheelchair in the trunk.

"Who is the next lucky contestant?" I asked Mom as she shut the back passenger door.

"I thought you could pick," Mom said to me with a grin.

"Are you kidding me?" I exclaimed. "It's Tommy Little, of course."

Tommy was my second favorite resident, after Grandma. He had been a chauffeur in Chicago for most of his adult life. I loved hearing him tell stories about living in a big city and about the lives of the wealthy people who employed him. His life had been so different from my boring existence in a small Iowa town.

Tommy's life took a drastic turn when he could no longer drive a limousine and was forced to retire. He lived in the city with his son for sometime. One day, his son suggested a road trip for the two of them. Somehow they ended up in Armstrong, Iowa, population eight hundred. Mr. Little's son signed him into the nursing home and relinquished what little income Tommy had to pay for his stay. His son left and was never seen or heard from again. I guess I am my mother's daughter because I quickly realized Tommy needed a family, so he became part of ours.

Mom and I appeared at Tommy's doorway. "You're spending Christmas at our house," I brashly informed him. I didn't even ask if he wanted to join us. He would have just said, "No, I don't want to impose." So I didn't give him that option. Tommy always dressed like a gentleman with a button down shirt, polyester slacks, and a belt. We helped him slip on his suit jacket, popped his newsboy hat on his head, and he looked like a prince headed to a ball.

"But I don't have a gift to bring," Tommy sputtered as we settled him in the backseat next to Princess Nettie.

"Shhh, you're the gift," I assured him. " Now get in the car and be on your best behavior." Then I shut the door before he could argue with me.

"We've got a seatbelt for one more in the backseat. Who is it going to be?" I questioned Mom.

"There are so many people here who need a family on Christmas. I just can't decide. I thought we could ask the nurses at the front desk to see who they would suggest," Mom answered.

That was a great idea. The nurses knew what we were up to because before loading each person in the car, we had to sign them out at the desk.

When we had the last person loaded in the backseat, I eased my way into the front on the driver's side and slid across the bench seat to the middle. I was relieved when Mom let me ride along. I thought maybe she was going to make me walk home, so she could squeeze one more senior citizen into the car. Mom took her place behind the wheel, and soon we were on our ten-minute journey across town to our home.

Initially, I had visions of our car being packed with elderly people with limbs and canes and walkers protruding from the windows. The car did feel like it was packed and ready to explode. But it wasn't from anything physical. It was filled with an intangible aura created by joy, happiness, and a healthy dose of Christmas spirit. It felt like we should open a few windows just to let some of the joy out.

We made the ten-minute trip in complete silence, but it wasn't uncomfortable. Our passengers were just too happy to talk. Periodically, I would glance in the rear view mirror to see three awe-inspiring smiles. What joy these people were experiencing by the simple fact that they were not forgotten on the most wonderful holiday of the year. Instead we had treated them like royalty-Grandma the Queen, Princess Nettie, and Prince Tommy. The situation made me realize that the greatest joy comes from the greatest need, but also when we give of our time and ourselves, we receive joy as well. It truly was a Christmas to remember. As the years passed, that particular Christmas became somewhat of a legend in our family. It was the holiday that all of us had been asked to guess who was coming to Christmas.

Reflections
• Because we are created in the likeness and image of God, each one of us should be loved and cherished, from the unborn fetus to the one hundred year old man or woman.
•Family has very little to do with DNA. It has everything to do with the bonds and relationships we create.

• Dad limited Mom to one carload full of people, but God found a way to reach beyond those boundaries. He gave us and our guests unlimited Christmas joy. God always finds a way to take limited situations and turn them into limitless possibilities.

•It wasn't the quantity of guests we invited to Christmas that was important, but the depth of the experience for each of us. Our guests found great joy because they had a great need. We experienced the joy from giving to others.

Grandma Mart and her great granddaughters

Janet Wong
from Hong Kong

"Be yourself because an original is worth more than a copy."

-Author Unknown

Although she was nineteen years old, Janet Wong looked like she was twelve. Not only was she very petite, but she also had the giggle of a middle school girl. Her dark, silky hair looked like someone had put a bowl upside down on her head and trimmed around the edges. Her wire-rimmed glasses framed her dark brown eyes. She had grown up as an only child in Hong Kong. Her father was a businessman, and her mother was a housewife. Although Janet was extremely intelligent, only the students who scored in the very top percentile on the country's high school exams were allowed to attend college in Hong Kong, so Janet's parents sent her to the United States to study business and computer science. That is how she became my roommate during my freshman year at Mankato State University in Minnesota.

Janet was a tiny, bird-like creature on the outside, but a powerhouse on the inside. I couldn't imagine coming to a foreign country alone at such a young age. As far as I was concerned, the girl had guts. Once she was settled into the dorm and had her class schedule down as a routine, Janet's next challenge was to obtain a car. This seemed a little odd because she didn't have a driver's license and had never owned or even driven a car. She explained to me that very few people owned cars where she lived. Most people, including her parents, relied on public transportation, and many people rode bicycles to their destinations. Very few students in our college dorms owned cars. We either walked or rode the city bus to get where we wanted to go. Janet didn't like those two options. She had a plan of her own.

Due to the time difference, she called her father at strange hours to discuss buying a car, and I was always in the room. I guess Janet didn't care if I heard their conversations because they were speaking in Chinese. Interestingly enough, I could tell a lot about their discussions just by the tone of Janet's voice. At times, they were arguing about the situation and at other moments, Janet would turn on her irresistible charm. In the end, it was clear she had her father wrapped around her little finger. Eventually, he sent her the money for a car. She ended up with a used, tan Ford escort. Our group of friends took turns giving her driving lessons. When I situated myself in the car with her on our first driving excursion, I was concerned she couldn't see over the dash and the steering wheel. I thought about getting a few pillows or textbooks for her to sit on, but we just kept adjusting the seat until she could see as well as reach the gas and brake pedals. We drove around the dorm parking lot to practice starting, stopping, and turning. Actually, Janet learned very quickly, and she had her driver's license in no time.

The semester seemed to fly by and soon there were only a few weeks until Christmas. I didn't want Janet to spend the holidays alone in our dorm room so I invited her to my parents' home in Iowa for Christmas. I must admit I was a little worried to introduce Janet, the little spitfire, to my mom who was no push over. Either these two women were going to get along famously, or it was going to be World War III. I had forgotten one factor. They both wanted to impress each other, so basically I had nothing to worry about or at least that is what I thought.

Janet and I both had finals to complete before we could start our journey to Iowa. We left the campus around noon. Janet was a pro at driving by now. She believed in putting the pedal to the metal, so we arrived at my parents' home in record-breaking time.

We brought in our suitcases, and I introduced Janet to Mom and Dad. Mom had just taken fresh baked chocolate chip cookies out of the oven. I poured four glasses of ice-cold milk to dip them in. While we enjoyed our delicious afternoon snack, my parents began asking Janet a series of questions about her family, where she grew up, and what she was studying. Janet graciously answered all their questions even though my mother was speaking in an extremely loud voice and at a very slow pace. It was annoying, and finally I couldn't take it any longer.

I grabbed the suitcases by the door and said, "Mom, why don't you show me where to put these?" I knew very well she wanted them in my bedroom, which was located in the back of the house. Once we were in the bedroom, I threw the suitcases on the bed and turned to face Mom.

"Ma, Janet is a very intelligent person. She speaks perfect English only with a Chinese accent, and she's certainly not deaf. Could you quit talking so loudly and so slowly to her?"

"I was just trying to be friendly," Mom responded in a voice that clearly told me she was insulted by my comment and question.

Mom and I followed the sound of Dad and Janet's laughter back to the kitchen. Dad was sharing a few of his corny jokes with our guest, and she was laughing hysterically. Mom continued to ask Janet questions in the loud, slow voice until finally it took too much energy to talk that way, and she began talking in her normal speaking voice. *Thank God*, I thought to myself.

Janet and I finished off the milk and cookies and then headed to my bedroom to unpack. When we emerged from the bedroom, I informed Mom we were going uptown to fill Janet's car with gas and to purchase some junk food. Janet and I both had a sweet tooth. The cookies hadn't satisfied our craving for sugar so we were in desperate need of a variety of candy bars.

When we returned, Mom was bustling about the kitchen making the evening meal. Janet joined Dad in the TV room, and I decided to help Mom in the kitchen. I sauntered over to the stove and gazed upon a frying pan filled with chicken stir-fry and a huge saucepan full of boiled, white rice.

My mother had never made stir-fry in her entire life. My parents lived and worked on a farm until they retired and moved to town. They ate farm food, which was meat and potatoes. My dad had suffered from a stomach ulcer most of his adult life. He did not eat spicy food, and he never tried anything new for fear it would irritate his ulcer. I could not imagine that he would eat this. Mom had it figured out. When we sat down at the table, the three ladies had plates full of delicious chicken stir-fry, while Dad had a couple of chicken breasts on a bed of rice. After supper, Janet and I helped Mom wash the dishes and clean up the kitchen. We all watched a little TV before going to bed.

The next morning, Janet and I wandered out to the kitchen to find Dad sitting at the kitchen bar by himself. Mom had gone uptown to run errands and pick up a few groceries.

"What are you eating, Mr. Wegner?" Janet questioned as she peered over his shoulder.

"Ah, this is my favorite breakfast. My mother used to make it for us when we were kids. Sometimes I like to eat it as a dessert. It's rice with a little cream, some raisins, and cinnamon sugar sprinkled on top. Do you girls want me to make some for you?"

Janet's right hand suddenly covered her mouth, and I honestly thought she was going to gag. I was pretty sure people in Hong Kong didn't eat rice with all the added ingredients Dad considered to be gourmet.

"Hey Janet, how about some Cheerios?" I inquired. She instantly gave me two thumbs up. I poured the cereal into two bowls, added the milk, and we enjoyed a simple yet tasty breakfast at the dining room table. There seemed to be a pattern that was forming, a pattern that centered around a four-letter word . . . rice. Maybe it was just a coincidence or maybe it stemmed from my mother's misconception that all Asian people eat rice at every meal. I decided to wait until after our next meal to make up my mind about this circumstance.

Janet and I spent the morning visiting my sisters who lived nearby. When we returned for lunch, Mom had steaming bowls of Spanish rice and a fresh tossed salad waiting for us. It was then I realized it was not a coincidence we were having rice at every meal.

After lunch I told Janet she didn't need to help us clean up because she was our guest. I sent her into the living room to enjoy watching TV with Dad. Once she was gone, Mom and I had another heart to heart talk.

"Mom, Janet does like rice, but she doesn't eat it at every meal. Could you make something else for a change?"

"I don't know why you have to be so picky. She's eaten everything I've made and never complained even once," Mom retorted.

"Of course, she isn't going to complain. She's too nice to do that. You are a great cook. Why don't you make some of your special dishes that we all love?" I asked.

"I can do that," Mom responded.

"And one more thing. I know what you are thinking, Mom. Do not ask Janet if she eats cats and dogs." Mother had the strange idea people from

Asia ate cats and dogs. She was constantly asking me if Janet dined on animals we considered pets.

"Well, does she?"

"No!"

"Okay, I was just wondering," Mom answered as she put the last of the dishes in the dishwasher.

I wandered into the living room to see Janet sitting on the sofa with her right hand placed firmly over her eyes. Her ring and middle fingers were spread apart forming a space for her left eye to peer through. I glanced from Janet to the TV. On the screen were two World Federation wrestlers pounding and jumping on each other. Dad was cheering them on from his recliner and not paying any attention to Janet.

"Dad, I don't think Janet is enjoying this," I stated.

"Sure she is. Aren't you, Janet?" he asked her.

"It is kind of violent, Mr. Wegner," Janet answered with her hand still plastered over her eyes.

"Come on, Janet. Let's go for a walk," I suggested.

Once we were bundled in our winter jackets, hats, scarves, and mittens, we headed down the street. The brisk Midwest air bit at our cheeks as I profusely apologized for my parents' behaviors. Mom had gone overboard with the rice while Dad was just his regular old self; telling corny jokes and watching his favorite redneck TV shows.

Janet assured me that there was no need to apologize. My parents were just trying to make her feel welcomed and comfortable. I looked at her.

How could someone who looked like they were twelve years old be so wise?

Mom took my words of advice to heart. That night for supper, we had her famous casserole made with hamburger, tomatoes and corn canned from her garden, and sliced potatoes. We sopped up the tomato juice with slices of buttered, fresh, homemade bread. Janet loved every bite. She kept telling Mother how delicious the food was, and that she had never tasted anything like it.

Soon it was Christmas Day. Janet attended early morning mass with us, and met many of our friends and neighbors. After we returned to my parents' home, my siblings began arriving with their families. When it came time for the big turkey dinner with all the fixings, I actually was able to eat upstairs with the adults because Janet was my guest. Normally, I would have been banished to the basement with the rest of the kids.

After the enormous meal, we waddled down to the basement for the gift exchange. We all had two gifts, one from the family name drawing and one from Mom and Dad. Because Mom was very thoughtful, she made sure Janet had two gifts as well. One gift was a gorgeous glass jewelry box with white orchids painted on the lid. It played a beautiful melody when you opened it. The other was a metal Christmas tin filled with homemade caramels, fudge, peanut clusters, and sugar cookies. It was the perfect gift for a petite Asian girl who had a big sweet tooth.

Janet had outdone herself with our gifts. Mom and I received blue velvet slippers decorated with beaded dragons. The slippers were so delicate and beautiful. I could never wear them because I regarded them as a work of art. My dad received a basket shaped like a turtle, which was about the size of a shoebox. It was filled with hard candies from Hong Kong. Janet had called her mother and asked her to send very special gifts for a very special family.

We all loved our gifts from the other side of the world, but the most treasured gift Janet gave us that Christmas was a simple lesson. If you want to impress someone, just be yourself. I had criticized Mom for trying to impress Janet, yet I had criticized Dad for being himself. I needed to let my parents be themselves. I needed to be proud of who they were.

God brings people in and out of our lives for a reason, and Janet was no exception. She taught me many lessons. She modeled courage, tenacity, and persistence for me. She changed my life forever. I will always be grateful for the friendship I shared with Janet, the time we spent together, and the memories we created. I will especially cherish the Christmas when she taught my entire family the importance of being yourself.

Reflections
•Be yourself.
•Don't judge people by what you see on the outside. It is what is on the inside that counts.
•God brings people in and out of our lives for a reason. It is all part of His plan for each of us to learn, grow, change, and become the people we are destined to become.

Home
for Christmas

"Family is not an important thing. It's everything."
                                        -Michael J. Fox

"Kevin can't make it home for Christmas," Mom stated in a robotic voice as she hung up the phone in the kitchen. It was as if she couldn't believe the words she has just spoken. Our entire family had always been home for Christmas. It was a tradition, not to be toyed with and certainly not to be broken.

My sister and I were sitting at the kitchen counter gazing at Mom in disbelief. We had both made it home for the beloved holiday. My sister, her husband, and their three children had driven from Omaha. On this particular day, her husband, Art, had taken their car and the kids to visit friends in town. I had made it home from college by sharing a ride with a friend in exchange for a tank of gas. My two older sisters and brother lived nearby with their families. They had only minutes to drive to reach our parents' home. It was Christmas Eve, and we were waiting on our last family member, our youngest brother, Kevin, to arrive from the small town about two hours away where he attended trade school.

Mom began to fill in the details regarding my brother's dilemma. "Kevin's car won't start and all of his roommates have already left for the holidays. To make matters worse something is

wrong with his furnace so his house has no heat."
I could tell by the tone of her voice that she was
not only disappointed but also extremely
worried.

   My sister and I glanced at each other. I guess
all those years of sharing a bedroom when we
were growing up, allowed us to read each other's
thoughts.

   " You thinkin' what I'm thinkin'?" I asked her.

   "Yep!" she replied as we simultaneously slid
off the kitchen bar stools and headed towards
the coat closet in the living room. Mom quickly
followed us, giving us the third degree.

   "What do you two think you are doing?" she
queried as we bundled ourselves in winter coats,
hats, boots, and gloves. She knew exactly what
we were doing, but the question had to be asked.

   "We're going to get Kevin, of course," I
answered.

   "That's crazy," she responded. "The biggest
storm of the year is supposed to be moving in
tonight."

   Unfortunately, that was true. Mom had a
small black and white TV on the kitchen counter
so she could watch soap operas while she
worked. We had the TV on throughout the day
while we baked Christmas cookies and prepared
food for our Christmas dinner. Mom's daytime
dramas had been continually interrupted by
weather updates about the incoming storm.
Several feet of snow were expected with blizzard

conditions and reduced visibility. Of course, a no travel warning was in effect.

Although not a single snowflake had fallen, large dark storm clouds had moved in across the Iowa plains. The temperature had quickly plummeted, and the wind had picked up from the west. When you've lived in the Midwest long enough, you can feel a storm coming in. "Feel it in your bones," is what my dad used to say. We didn't need some weather person on TV to tell us a storm was coming. We could feel it. It was an eerie, mysterious, impending feeling of doom. It was as if we were waiting for a monster to arrive. We didn't know what the monster would look like or when it would arrive, but we knew it was coming.

"I can see that you two have your minds made up, but I wish you wouldn't go," Mom implored.

"If we leave now we might be able to get ahead of the storm," Mary assured Mom as we headed for the door that led to the garage.

"We'll be fine," I added as we both gave Mom a goodbye hug.

Crisp, cold air stung our faces when we entered the garage. It was five in the afternoon, so Dad had already left for his shift as the night watchman at the local factory. The side of the garage where his old, beat up pickup truck was usually parked was empty. On the side of the garage that was closest to the house sat our mode of transportation, our parents' big, blue, four-doored Chrysler. We often referred to it as

"The Boat." When in reality it was more like a battleship. The huge car engulfed the garage space. When we looked at the enormous vehicle, we could sense the very essence of its power.

"I'll drive," my sister blurted out as she opened the door on the driver's side of the car.

"I call shotgun," I replied as I slipped into the passenger seat.

Mary started the engine, and then gunned it as a precautionary measure just to make sure it was running smoothly. She pushed the button on the garage door opener, we backed into the driveway, and then she closed the garage door. There was no going back now.

Mom was standing at the living room bay window reluctantly waving goodbye. I could understand her concern. Now, instead of having one child to worry about, she had three.

As we cruised down Main Street, we realized the first leg of our journey was fairly simple. The population of our hometown was approximately eight hundred people. We often joked about the fact that when you were in high school, it was difficult to find someone to date that wasn't your cousin. Needless to say, in a town that size there were no traffic lights, only a few stop signs. Once out of town, we took the highway, and that's when our real journey began.

The car was soon filled with the melodies of Christmas carols. After several rounds of "Frosty the Snowman" and "Silent Night," an hour had passed, and the snow had begun to fall. Not only had the weather changed dramatically, but so had our mood. Our cheerful Christmas carols had turned into the stressful recitation of the decades of the rosary. The sound of "Our Fathers" and "Hail Marys" now filled the car on the inside as the snow swirled around us on the outside.

In a matter of minutes, a few snowflakes had transformed into a wall of white. The monster had arrived. As the sun set, and it became dark, the visibility had decreased considerably. Mary was a careful driver so she had decreased the speed of the car. It was a necessary tactic, but it felt like we were crawling down the highway. Reaching our destination seemed impossible.

The wind howled reminding us of the hideous monster's arrival. Although we were frightened, we decided to gang up on the beast. We couldn't tell if we were on the road or not, so I watched for the painted line on the shoulder, and Mary watched for the dotted line in the center of the highway. There were no tire tracks to follow since no one else was on the road. I guess everyone had actually heeded the travelers' advisory warning and stayed in their safe, cozy homes. Not us. We were on a mission to save our brother from a fate worse than death . . . spending Christmas alone.

Visibility was zero. Mary had tried both the high and low headlights but neither helped her to see any better. Since no other cars were on the highway, we gave up our plan of staying in our lane and simply drove smack dab in the middle of the road. We wanted to keep plenty of distance between the car and the road ditch.

Even with the wipers on high, we couldn't keep the windshield clean. The heavy, wet, sloppy snow kept accumulating on the glass and wipers. Every few minutes, we would count to three then roll down our windows. The screaming wind blew sheets of snow into the Chrysler, quickly sweeping the air we needed to breathe past our faces. Each of us would hold our breath as we reached out the window, grabbed a wiper, and let it slap against the windshield, shattering the ice from the rubber blades. Then we quickly rolled up the windows, looked at each other, and screamed at the top of our lungs. We thought about stopping to scrape the windows, but we were concerned we would never get started again. With no one else on the road to help us, stopping was a very dangerous proposition. Simply put, it was us against the monster storm. As the battle raged, we continued to pray out loud, but we gave up the idea of praying the structure of the rosary, and said prayers randomly.

The monster had hit us with all of its dangerous weapons. The snow had decreased our vision. The ice had decreased our traction, and now snowdrifts detoured our journey like giant speed bumps. Mary would plow into the drifts causing huge chunks of snow to hit the windshield, slide over the top of the car, and crash onto the road behind us. Each time she would impale a gigantic drift, we would interrupt our prayers with frightened heartfelt screams. With everything the monstrous storm had thrown at us, we never thought of turning back. We had a mission. We had come too far to turn back now, and the competitive side in both of us was emerging. It was us against the storm, and we were determined to win. When we finally arrived at our brother's house, we did feel a sense of victory, but we also knew our journey was only half complete because we still had to drive home.

We pulled into the driveway of Kevin's house, ran to the door, and rushed inside without bothering to knock. The inside temperature was a little warmer than the outside, but not much. I could see my breath when I exhaled. That wasn't a good sign. Even though the temperature was cold, our brother greeted us with a warm hello.

Kevin had his suitcase packed and sitting by the door. It was plain to see that he was eager to leave. We were as well, but it was late, and we had expended a lot of emotional energy just getting there. We were famished.

"Do you have anything to eat?" I questioned as I headed for the kitchen. A quick glance inside the empty refrigerator answered that question. What little food was in the refrigerator was covered with hairy, blue and green mold. The contents looked more like science experiments than something you would eat. Mother would have been shocked if she would have known that Kevin had no car, no heat, and no food! Mary and I settled for a glass of water from the tap instead of a quick snack. Besides Mom would have steaming bowls of oyster stew waiting for us when we arrived home. We all hated oyster stew, but we ate it every Christmas Eve without complaining because it was a family tradition.

"You two ready to go?" asked my brother. "Who's going to drive?"

"You can," my sister and I chimed in unison as we quickly glanced at each other.

"We're tired from the trip here, so you can take over at the wheel," Mary added.

Kevin grabbed his suitcase, threw it in the trunk, and the three of us piled into the front seat. Fortunately, the old blue Chrysler "battleship" had a bench seat in the front with plenty of room, and no one wanted to sit in the cold back seat alone. We wanted to be warm and toasty and together in the front. In fact, wasn't that the purpose of the entire trip . . .being together for Christmas?

Even though the weather on the way home was worse, the trip was better. Just by having Kevin in the car with us, we felt we had completed our mission. There is always something about Kevin that calms everyone around him. Perhaps it is his easygoing demeanor, his slow, steady monotone voice that registers just above a whisper. Perhaps it is the fact that he faces problems head on without a trace of emotion or stress on the outside, but who knows what may be churning on the inside.

Each time he crashed through a snowdrift, he would keep on talking as if chunks of snow and ice sailing over the car was an everyday occurrence. It was quite a different experience from his sisters' shrill screams on the journey to his house. Periodically, Kevin would roll down the driver's side window to snap the ice off the wiper blades. There was no counting to three or screaming involved as we had done on the trip to rescue him. He kept on talking in his low monotone voice as if to calm our fears. It made me think just who was rescuing whom?

Soon, we were pulling into our parents' driveway. The tune "I'll Be Home for Christmas" echoed in my head. Truly the words Bing Crosby so beautifully crooned now had new meaning for my entire family.

We had arrived home victorious. We had snatched our brother from the monstrous storm. I don't know if we were motivated that night by fear, bravery, stupidity, or love. Perhaps, it was a little of each.

Kevin carefully parked the old, blue Chrysler "battleship" in the garage. The three of us entered the house and stomped the snow from our boots on the plastic mat in front of the door. Mom greeted us with hugs. We had given her a precious gift that she would remember and cherish for the rest of her life. It wasn't a gift that would fit in a Christmas stocking or a gift box. The gift was that we were all together for Christmas.

   We removed our boots, and sauntered into the dining room where bowls of steaming, creamy, white oyster stew awaited us. It was good to be home.

<u>Reflections</u>
•Sometimes in life you need to know when to be persistent and not give up.
•Just being together can be a gift.
•When the monster storms in life rage around you, find comfort in the old, blue Chrysler otherwise known as God's love. There's nothing fancy about it, but it's always there, always reliable. It will always keep you safe from the storm.

Our family's home in Armstrong, Iowa

Christmas
in an Elk Herd

"Why fit in when you were born to stand out?"
                                        -Dr. Seuss

"We can't come home for Christmas," my sister Mary stated in a sad, monotone voice over the phone.

"Why not?" I queried.

"Art is working on a special project. You know, the kind where he says, 'I could tell you what I'm working on, but then I'd have to kill you,' " Mary explained.

I had to admit I did love Art's sense of humor. Mary's husband, Art, had joined the Navy right out of high school. Once out of the Navy, he earned his bachelor's degree in engineering then joined the Air Force. His previous experience in the Navy, his degree, and his maturity made him "hot stuff" in the Air Force. All joking aside, he probably was working on some top-secret project.

"Art is only going to have a few days off around Christmas, which means we don't have enough time to travel home," Mary shared in a depressed tone.

This was the year that Mary really needed to come home for the holidays. She had expressed to me on several occasions that she just didn't seem to fit in where they had been assigned. I was truly shocked by this information. Their family had lived on Navy and Air Force bases throughout the United States. Through these experiences, they had met many people who became their lifelong friends.

I have always felt there is an unwritten, unspoken code between families who have a member in the military. Military members are forced to live nomadic lives by the very nature of their careers. Of course, their families become nomads as well, living on bases all over the world. These families usually live away from grandparents, aunts, uncles, and cousins. So out of necessity, military families become close friends with other military families. It makes sense because they have so much in common.

Knowing each assignment is temporary causes military families to skip the social niceties of getting to know your neighbors. Once you met your neighbors, you were instantly friends. When a moving truck pulled up to a home in base housing, neighbors were immediately at your door asking the ages of your kids, where your last assignment was, and how many years did you have until retirement. Of course, they would bring a casserole and a dozen chocolate chip cookies for your first evening meal in your new home.

This was not the case when my sister and her family moved to base housing at their current location. No one showed up at their door to greet them. In fact, the neighborhood seemed deserted. Mary knew people lived in the houses, yet she never saw a single soul. While Art headed off to work each day and their two daughters, Michelle and Allison, went to school, Mary was left at home with their preschool-aged son, Shane. Granted, Shane was a sweet boy, but at the ripe old age of four, he was rambunctious and not much of a conversationalist. Needless to say, Mary was off the scale in terms of loneliness.

"We'll just have Christmas here," Mary's voice echoed over the phone.

"Don't worry. We'll think of something," I assured her.

"But it's not your problem," she argued.

But it was my problem. Mary was a unifying force in our family. She always thought of others before herself. She constantly made sacrifices for her husband, children, our parents, and siblings. Now in her time of need, it was our turn to give back to her.

After our phone conversation, I took a few days to think about the situation, and I eventually came up with a possible solution. Throughout my life, when I hatched a crazy idea, I called my older sister, Barb, for a healthy dose of wisdom, logic, and advice. So that is exactly what I did. Not only did Barb love my solution, but she wanted to join me in my endeavor. If Mary couldn't come home for Christmas, we would bring Christmas to her. Of course, we couldn't bring our entire family, but we could bring a sampling of family members (Barb and me). Barb had one son who was married and on his own. Her husband was a bit of a scrooge who didn't enjoy Christmas. I was single and living in Minneapolis. So it seemed logical that we were the perfect pair to represent our family at Mary's Christmas gathering.

I called Mary to explain our devious plan. I expected her to talk me out of traveling to her home, but I was pleasantly surprised when she was excited and overjoyed to have Barb and me as Christmas guests. She asked what we would like to do on our visit. Knowing Mary loved a good challenge, I told her to surprise us.

I now had another challenge facing me. How was I going to get Barb on a commercial plane? Actually, I don't think it was the plane that frightened her. It was the airport. Barb hated two things commonly found in airports . . . crowds and escalators. I felt we were two intelligent women who could deal with these fears. When it came to crowds, I told Barb to just concentrate on me. As far as we were concerned, it was just the two of us, and no one else mattered. As for the escalator phobia, we would just avoid them at all costs. Once we arrived at the Minneapolis airport, we checked our bags, and headed to our assigned gate. We took an elevator, several flights of stairs, and a couple of moving sidewalks, and eventually we reached our gate without setting foot on one single escalator.

Our flight was uneventful, and before we knew it, we were landing. This was at a time when people could meet you at your arrival gate, which was exactly what Mary and her family did. There were joyous hugs for everyone before we headed to the luggage claim area. Barb was at the front of the pack, visiting with the kids. Mary and I lagged behind so I could remind her about Barb's fear of escalators. Mary had remembered and already had a plan. I should have known she would. She was always thinking of others.

We grabbed our luggage from the twirling carousel and headed to the parking garage. After stuffing our suitcases into the trunk, Barb and I squeezed into the backseat with the kids. It was fun being physically and emotionally close as we drove to the Air Force base. The kids were eager to tell us about their new home and new schools, so the time in the car passed quickly.

As we turned into the entrance of base housing, I looked out of the car window and was shocked by the dismal look and feel of the neighborhood. The houses were a tired beige color with white trim, white doors, and white carports. It was a winter evening so no one was on the streets or sidewalks. That was no surprise. Usually, on cold winter evenings, people are safely tucked away in their homes, but you can see in through the windows of their homes as if you are taking a quick glimpse of their lives. You might see a family watching television or enjoying the evening meal at the dinner table. But in this neighborhood, every house had the blinds or curtains closed, signaling to those passing by to stay out of their lives. The entire environment seemed dark, dreary, and uninviting. I could understand why Mary didn't feel comfortable here. I wouldn't either.

This seemed like such a stark contrast to the other places they had lived. I remembered their assignment at the Navy base in Long Beach, California. Art was on a destroyer off the coast of Vietnam. He was halfway around the globe in a dangerous situation while Mary lived in base housing with their oldest daughter, who was a preschooler at the time. Of course, Mary was worried about her husband, and she began to develop a bad case of loneliness. I was in high school at the time, and somehow I convinced my parents to allow me to spend summer break with Mary in California.

When I arrived, I was amazed at the hustle and bustle of the neighborhood. Of course, there were very few men in sight. All of them were sailors who had been deployed to Vietnam. The women would sit in groups on their front porches watching their children ride their bicycles, tricycles, and scooters up and down the sidewalks. Periodically, a mom would drag out a garden hose and attach a sprinkler to it. This was an open invitation to all the neighborhood kids to come and run through the squirting water, screaming and laughing in pure delight.

Each of these amazing women had a husband who was fighting a war overseas. This common bond, this common fear for their spouses' lives, made their friendships very tight. If they weren't sitting on their porches watching their children play outdoors, they were gathered in each other's kitchens to share news about their husbands, and to release some emotions fueled by fear and worry. They were all about being together and helping each other. The neighborhood on base housing in Long Beach had a happy, comforting buzz about it. From the moment you set foot on one of the grassy lawns, you knew you were among friends.

Truly, Mary's current neighborhood and the Naval base in California were polar opposites. I realized it was a cold December evening when we arrived, and that was a factor into why no one was out and about, but when morning arrived the next day, not much had changed except for the daylight.

It was Saturday morning, and we were all rejoicing in the fact that Art didn't have to work. Mary, in her infinite wisdom, had decided that if there was any fun in our near future, we were going to need to leave the base. Little Shane was willing to give up his Saturday morning cartoons in exchange for a new adventure. His sisters, Michelle and Allison, were more than happy to go anywhere with their visiting aunts. So we bundled up in winter clothing, packed ourselves into the car, and headed to the nearest ski slope.

Being from the plains of the Midwest, Barb and I were mesmerized by the beauty and grandeur of the Rocky Mountains. While Barb and I continued to appreciate the gorgeous scenery by gazing out of the car windows, Michelle and Allison filled us in on their school activities and busy social lives.

As we were unloading the car in the parking lot of the ski resort, Barb informed us that she wouldn't be skiing today. She would hang out in the lodge to enjoy some prime time people watching. This was no surprise to the rest of us. This was a woman who was deathly afraid of escalators so there was no way she was going to ski down the side of a mountain. Mary quickly volunteered to stay with Barb in the warm, comfy lodge. This was all part of the plan Barb and I had developed.

Even though Art was the one in the military, Barb and I were up to a little espionage of our own. Of course, Barb wasn't going skiing, and we decided to use that to our advantage. We knew Mary would volunteer to stay in the lodge with her because that is the kind of person Mary was. She was always thinking of others. Barb's job was to find out more about Mary's emotional state. I, on the other hand, was supposed to find out more about the situation from Art and the kids while trying to stay alive on the dangerous slopes of the ski area. I think Barb got the better end of that deal.

Art, the kids, and I headed to the counter to rent our skis and boots. In the process, the person behind the desk asked if we wanted to take ski lessons.

"I am a flatlander who has only skied once, and it wasn't a positive experience," I admitted. "I can't imagine that 'Mr. Hot Rod' (referring to Shane the preschooler) knows how to ski."

Art chuckled.

"What's so funny?" I asked.

"It's just the fact that you think 'Mr. Hot Rod' can stand still long enough for a ski lesson, let alone listen to the instructor," Art replied. "I do think it would be a good idea for all of us to take a lesson."

Art paid for our gear and lessons, then the five of us strapped on our boots, grabbed our skis, and stomped toward the area outside designated as The Ski School.

Art was right about Shane. He was having a difficult time staying upright on skis. He was either clinging to his dad's leg for stability, or he was sprawled on the ground. Fortunately, our instructor had an easy solution for this problem. He simply connected the tips of Shane's skis with a three-inch, brown, rubber hose. This prevented Shane's skis from going in opposite directions causing him to do the splits and crash to the ground. The instructor informed us of an added bonus to the rubber hose. By having the tips of the skis point at each other, the outside ski edges would form a "V." The edges would rub against the snow causing friction, and the friction would decrease Shane's speed. This was a move known as the snowplow. I quickly stashed the snowplow information away in my memory, not only for Shane's safety, but also for my own.

Soon, we had successfully completed our ski lesson, so we headed to the chairlift, which would take us to the run commonly referred to as "The Bunny Hill," but for me, it might as well have been the summit of Mount Everest.

Once I dismounted from the chairlift, I slowly and carefully used my ski poles to push off and start the descent down the Bunny Hill. My speed increased, and I kept thinking, *Snowplow! Snowplow!* as I attempted to point the tips of my skis towards each other. I was a quarter of the way down the hill when Shane whizzed by me using his poles to push himself so he could go even faster. His dad was a few yards behind him yelling, "Slow down! You're going too fast."

On our next trek down the slope, Art decided to take Shane's ski poles away from him in an effort to slow him down a little. Once again, I was a quarter of the way down the slope when little Shane sped by me in a blur of color.

I didn't think Shane was racing down the hill on purpose. He just knew the goal of skiing was to start at the top of the slope and end at the bottom.

No one had told him there was a particular speed he had to use to accomplish this goal. As I watched him glide by me one more time, I felt myself wishing I could ski more like the little mite. His skiing style was smooth, wild, and carefree. On the other hand, my skiing style was more like having the hiccups. I would ski a few yards then lose control and do a face plant in the snow. I would use my ski poles to stand, then the entire process would start all over. This was very frustrating and time consuming. The Bradley family members were making two runs to one of mine. As I watched Shane zip past me again, I realized what I was doing wrong. My fear of falling was actually making me fall. It was a self-fulfilling prophecy.

During the chairlift ride back up the slope, I decided there was nothing to fear. If I fell, the only thing that would be injured was my pride. I visualized taking my fear and making it into a snowball, which I threw into the nearby forest. Next, I imagined myself soaring down the slope like a graceful hawk skimming the surface of the snow.

On my next run, I didn't exactly soar down the hill, but I did manage to make it down the slope without falling, crashing, or face planting. My sense of accomplishment must have been evident because my nieces cheered when I reached the bottom. I made a few more runs in an effort to replace my "crash and burn" style of skiing with something a bit more graceful.

Time seemed to fly by as quickly as Shane was flying down the hill. Soon, it was time for lunch. We removed our skis, set them by the side of the lodge along with our poles, and with our ski boots on, we clunked inside.

We found Mary and Barb sitting at a table near the huge two story picture window, which faced the mountain. The view was spectacular. We deposited Shane beside his mother, then headed to the restaurant to fill several trays with delicious food and steaming mugs of hot chocolate.

Our morning skiing escapades, along with a tasty hot meal had given our egos a boost, so after lunch we decided to tackle the green circle slope, which was slightly more difficult than the Bunny Hill. I hadn't been successful on my top secret, fact-finding mission during the morning ski runs. It was somewhat difficult to carry on a conversation when your face is buried in the snow. Since I was feeling more confident about my skiing abilities, I had high hopes for the afternoon in terms of collecting information about how the Bradley family was adjusting to their new environment. I decided to concentrate on the chairlift. Each time I miraculously made it to the bottom of the slope, I would hook up with a different family member in the chair lift line.

I found out from the chairlift conversations that everyone was struggling with adapting to their new environment, but it was particularly difficult for Mary. She was sad and depressed, which was the exact opposite of her normally happy, bubbly personality.

It was late in the afternoon when we decided we had skied enough for the day. We turned in our equipment and packed ourselves into the car. On the way home, we went thru a fast food drive up for hamburgers, fries, and sodas. Skiing must have burned a lot of calories because not only were we starving, but also exhausted. We ate our "gourmet" meal in the car, devouring the burgers, and slurping the sodas in elated ecstasy.

When we arrived back at the house, it was dark. We were tired from a day jam-packed with physical activity, so we put on our pajamas and collapsed into our beds.

We awoke the next morning to the excitement of it being the day before Christmas. There was a magical, electric vibe in the air as we spent the day baking Christmas cookies, cleaning the house, and putting the finishing touches on a few last minute gifts.

I was surprised that over the course of the last several days, no one from the neighborhood had showed up at the door with a plate of Christmas goodies accompanied by a healthy dose of holiday greetings and Christmas cheer. I suggested that we wrap up some of the treats we had created and deliver them to the neighbors.

"Not a good idea," Mary informed me. "Most of the neighbors have gone back to their hometowns to spend the holidays with their families and friends."

"I guess that means there will be more for us to enjoy," I responded as the kids cheered, realizing there would be more cookies for them to devour.

That evening instead of dining on the dreaded oyster stew our mother forced us to eat every Christmas Eve, Mary served a pan of her famous enchiladas. We topped off the delicious meal with the delightful Christmas cookies we had created together.

With our stomachs full, the gifts wrapped, and the stockings hung, it seemed like there was nothing left to do but go to bed and wait for the arrival of Santa Claus. That's what the kids thought, but the adults knew there was one more task to complete. After the kids were tucked safely in their beds, Art went to the carport to retrieve a box containing bicycle parts. Mary and Art had purchased a bike for Shane's Christmas gift, but it needed to be assembled. Mary, Barb, and I organized the bicycle parts on the kitchen floor while Art organized the tools. The sister trio tried to help by reading the instruction manual, but we soon realized bicycle assembly was meant to be a one man job, and that one man was Art. So the ladies headed off to bed leaving the Air Force officer sitting on the kitchen floor surrounded by bike parts, tools, and a plate of Christmas cookies.

That evening Barb and I were finally alone so we could share what we each had found out on our fact-finding missions. Even though we had collected the information from different sources, we came to the same conclusion . . . the entire family was struggling with adapting to their new surroundings, but it had been especially difficult for Mary. We both agreed we had made the right choice in coming to their home for Christmas. Our visit was good for the Bradley family. It was also good for us to have a change of scenery and to have the opportunity to be with our beloved sister. We were all happy for the time being, but we wondered what would happen once we left. We had no idea how to help Mary after Christmas, other than increasing our phone calls to her. We would have to keep thinking and simply enjoy our time together this Christmas.

Christmas morning was filled with excitement and anticipation. Shane was up before the sun. The kids opened their gifts from Santa while still in their pajamas. After the tornado of wrapping paper, ribbons, and gifts subsided, we all dressed, popped the turkey into the oven, and went to mass.

The aroma of roasted turkey greeted us when we returned to the house. We changed into our casual clothes before heading to the kitchen to help prepare our Christmas feast. While Michelle and Allison set the table, Mary boiled the potatoes and conjured up lump-free gravy. Barb and I were in charge of salads and side dishes. Shane played with his new toys while Art enjoyed watching sports on TV, until it was time to carve the turkey.

It was a cozy gathering of seven happy people compared to the crowd of over thirty relatives who celebrated Christmas at our parents' home each year. After we had stuffed ourselves with the delicious food, cleared the table, and cleaned the kitchen, we headed to the living room to power lounge on the sofas and recliners. Although the gifts from Santa had already been opened, we still had our gifts for each other to exchange. Michelle and Allison quickly took on the role of elves, sorting through the gifts and piling the presents at each person's feet.

There were shirts and funky socks for Michelle and Allison. Shane was overjoyed with his collection of new toys. Art appreciated the causal shirts he would wear when he wasn't sporting his Air Force uniform. Mary had made decorative craft items for our homes. Of course, the three sisters loved receiving our favorite perfumes and candles.

After opening our gifts, we called the relatives who had gathered at our parents' home in Iowa. Fun conversations about gifts and news from our hometown followed. Even though we were hundreds of miles away from our traditional Christmas gathering, for a few fleeting moments, it felt like we were all together for the holidays.

Once we ended the phone conversation, I sat on the sofa surrounded by newly opened gifts, crumpled wrapping paper, an assortment of ribbons and bows, and the happy faces of Mary, Art, and their kids. It was then I realized it wasn't the gifts that were important; it was the fact we were together. That was the greatest gift. I realized there was an unwritten, unspoken code between military families, and there was also an unwritten, unspoken code between my family members. We had each other's backs. Not only did we celebrate the good times in life, but we also helped each other through the tough times as well. No matter what the physical distance between us was, we would always be close. Our sisterhood was a pact based on the fact that we would always be there for each other. This Christmas trip was the perfect example. Mary needed us, so without question or hesitation, we came to be with her and her family to help in any way we could. I felt good about helping my sister, and I also felt comforted by knowing I would never be alone. My sisters would always be there for me.

With a peaceful glow on my face, I stuffed the ripped wrapping paper, ribbons and bows into the familiar black trash bag that once held Shane's new bike. For the remainder of the afternoon, we played board games and cards while Shane rode his new bike complete with training wheels around the house. When the sun began to set, we created delicious turkey sandwiches complete with creamy mayo, crisp lettuce leaves, and slices of Swiss cheese. After watching the movie *It's a Wonderful Life*, we headed to bed knowing it had been a wonderful day.

We awoke realizing it would be our last full day together. The sun glowed in a cloudless sky. The icicles on the roof began to drip and decrease in size. The snow morphed from a solid to a liquid. The melting snow created small rivers and streams in the gutters of the neighborhood streets. We took the warm weather as an opportunity to be outside. We walked through the neighborhood accompanied by Shane on his new bike. Shane was overjoyed by the fact he could ride his bike outside rather than inside the house, and so were we.

Although the physical atmosphere of the community was sunny and warm, the emotional atmosphere was icy and cold. There were no cars in the streets or people on the sidewalks. The closed curtains and blinds created the eerie atmosphere of a ghost town. We created our own fun by making snowballs and hurling them at each other. When we returned to the house, we built a jovial snowman on the front lawn. We had decided if we couldn't find a friendly neighbor, then at least we could make a snowy one.

Art returned home from work early. That's when we knew something was up. Mary and Art had one more surprise planned for the "flatland" sisters. We packed ourselves into the car and headed to an undisclosed destination. We soon realized we were heading towards the mountains. As the sun neared the horizon, we found ourselves surrounded by enormous pine trees of a national forest. We turned off the highway into a large parking area. Art exited the car and headed for a small cabin near the edge of the parking lot. He returned in a few minutes and informed us, "We are all set."

All set for what? We still had no idea what we were doing in a forest at sunset. We were up for a new adventure so we piled out of the car and followed Art single file on a trail through the gigantic, evergreen trees. Soon the trees thinned, and we found ourselves in a clearing where several horse drawn sleighs were waiting. Two of the sleighs were overflowing with hay. The other sleighs were clearly meant for human passengers. Fortunately, we all fit into one sleigh. We covered ourselves with lap blankets, the driver snapped the reins across the backs of the two large horses, which were hitched to the sleigh, and our adventure began. We followed a trail through several stands of trees and many clearings.

Our sleigh suddenly came to a stop at the edge of the forest. As we gazed at the clearing in front of us, we realized we had reached our destination. The magical scene before us took my breath away. The sun had painted the sky and looming snow-capped mountains a glowing orange. As the sun set, the temperature dropped and icicles began forming on the nearby evergreen boughs. The snow in the clearing sparkled like diamonds. Amidst all the beauty was a majestic herd of elk. The sleigh driver cautioned us to be quiet as we continued our journey into the brown sea of mountain mammals. A sleigh filled with hay orbited our sleigh, dropping hay in a circle around us. The elk surrounded us as they munched on their evening meal. Dark brown hair covered the massive elk bodies. Puffs of frozen moisture streamed from their nostrils. We sat in a trance-like state, mesmerized by the beauty of the spectacular beasts.

Sitting in a sleigh in the middle of an elk herd surrounded by the majestic Rocky Mountains was an experience beyond my imagination. I glanced at Mary to thank her for the fabulous adventure she had provided for us. When I glanced at my sweet sister's face with hundreds of elk in the background, the answer I had been so desperately searching for came to me. Even though we were enjoying the beauty and mystic of the elk, it didn't mean we wanted to be one of them. You can enjoy and appreciate your surroundings without assimilating into it. We all need to stay true to ourselves. Even though my sister had found herself in an unwelcoming environment, that didn't mean she needed to change who she was to fit into "the herd."

Once the kids were asleep in their beds that evening, I sat with Mary at the kitchen table and shared my epiphany in the elk herd with her. She wanted desperately to remain her positive, happy self, but due to the environment, which surrounded her, it was a daily struggle. She thanked me for bringing happiness to what could have been a dismal Christmas. We hugged for a long time, almost unwilling to let each other go, knowing letting go was a symbol of us each going our separate ways in the morning when Barb and I left to fly back to the Midwest.

Shortly after our departure, Mary wisely decided to seek help from a doctor for depression. Medication, counseling, and knowing that their current assignment was not their permanent home, helped Mary survive the situation. I admired her for knowing when it was time to seek help from outside sources.

Later in my life, when I suffered from severe depression, I felt like I was trapped in a dark hole and each time I tried to claw my way out, the sides of the hole simply caved in on me making the situation worse. It was the hand of my beloved sister, Mary, who reached down into that hole and pulled me out. Once again, she showed me you can't always do everything yourself. She showed me the importance of helping each other. I thought about the life lesson I had learned about being true to yourself no matter what environment surrounds you. I would have never imagined it would be a lesson I would learn by spending Christmas in an elk herd.

Reflections

•You can appreciate your environment, but you don't need to become "part of the herd" to fit in. Remain true to yourself.

•It's important to know when you can solve problems yourself and when to ask for help.

•There is an unwritten, unspoken code between all families in knowing the members will always be there to celebrate the good times, and to help each other through the challenges.

The Bradley Family

My First Christmas Tree

"When you are down to nothing, God is up to something."   -Author Unknown

My heart was pounding wildly in my chest. I wasn't sure if it was from the physical effort of tugging and pushing the freshly cut Christmas tree through the front door, or the emotions of having my first Christmas tree in my own apartment.

I was proud and elated to have landed my first teaching job in Sioux Falls, South Dakota. As the ultimate act of independence, I rented a small one-bedroom apartment by myself . . . no roommates. My new residence was a cozy, basement apartment in an old, white, fourplex, and it was mine, all mine.

With one last push, the tree popped through the apartment door with a scraping sound, depositing small, green needles across the tan, shag carpet. I didn't mind. I could easily clean the needles up later. I stopped to catch my breath and to enjoy the fresh smell of pine that had permeated the room.

Once the tree was inside the apartment, I needed to conquer the next challenge, which was where to put a six-foot evergreen tree in a very limited space. I quickly surveyed the apartment. Each room had minimal furniture, which made the space appear larger than it actually was. The bedroom contained a single bed I had purchased from a thrift store, and a chest of drawers salvaged from my parents' basement. The kitchen and dining room melded into one space. A tablecloth I had constructed from material found in my mother's quilting scraps covered the small folding table and all of its imperfections. Three dark, wooden chairs that I had inherited from my grandmother surrounded the table. The living area was scantily furnished with a couch, one swiveling chair, and a TV, which stately occupied a spot on top of a small coffee table.

The sparsely furnished living room seemed to be the logical new home for my majestic tree. I tugged the tree to the corner of the room, and dropped the tree stand and a string of lights beside it. I knew in a matter of minutes, I would have this beautiful evergreen in an upright position. I methodically turned the bolts of the metal tree stand into the rough, brown bark. The sap stuck to my fingers like glue, but I enjoyed the syrup-like texture and color, as well as the pine smell that continued to fill the small apartment.

I jostled the tree into the selected corner of the room then stepped back to admire my treasure. I loved how its branches reached out and up to the ceiling, claiming the space in the room as if it were royalty. I loved the fresh, clean, pine smell, and how the needles scraped my skin when I touched it. When I closed my eyes, I could imagine myself in the middle of an evergreen forest instead of a basement apartment on the Dakota plains. Being the first Christmas season on my own, the tree provided me with what I needed . . . a huge dose of Christmas spirit.

Obviously, the tree took up a big chunk of space in my living room, but I had room to spare. It also took a big chunk out of my budget. Unfortunately, I didn't have money to spare. Beginning teachers always have and probably always will live at the poverty level. By the time I paid my rent, utilities, car and student loan payments, I barely had money for food. My diet consisted mainly of macaroni and cheese. Occasionally, I would splurge on a can of spam or a package of processed bologna. I had actually skipped a few meals over the last few months to save money for the tree. When that didn't seem like enough, I turned down the heat to cut back on the cost of utilities. It seemed like a simple solution to just wear my coat in the apartment and throw an extra quilt on my bed at night. After purchasing the tree and the necessary accessories, which included the metal tree stand and one string of lights, I had no money left to buy ornaments, but I had a plan brewing in my head to solve that problem.

The Lord had blessed me with the gifts of creativity and resourcefulness. These gifts were often utilized in my work as an elementary school art teacher. I was in charge of all the bulletin boards in the hallways of the school. On one hand, it was great because I always had space to display the students' artwork. On the other hand, it was a lot of work. I changed the boards every four weeks. I would usually stay after school to switch the displays. When I took the art projects off a bulletin board, I would put the pieces on each teacher's desk so she could return them to the students to take home. At the end of November when it was time to change the bulletin boards from Thanksgiving projects to Christmas artwork, I decided to take an empty garbage bag with me. My plan was when I entered each classroom to put the November projects on the teacher's desk; I would check the trashcan for any scraps of construction paper.

All the adults had spoken to the children about recycling, and the kids really took those words to heart because there weren't many scraps of construction paper being thrown away. I was lucky enough to find two used spiral notebooks in a trashcan. I ripped off the covers because the inside front cover was white and could be used just like tagboard. Crazy as it may seem, I felt like I had hit a jackpot in Vegas.

Later that evening after dinner, I dumped the contents of the trash bag onto the dining room table. I picked out the treasured notebook covers first. I carefully drew the holy family including baby Jesus, Mary, and Joseph on the tagboard. I meticulously added color and life to the figures using crayons. I cut each one out separately and glued a tagboard strip to the back so that each figure could stand in an upright position. I managed to use the remaining tagboard to create two kneeling shepherds and three, fluffy, white sheep. Unfortunately, there was not enough tagboard for the three wise men, let alone their large, hairy camels.

After placing the figures under the tree to form a nativity scene, I surveyed my masterpiece. Someone else's trash had become my treasure. All I needed to add was a little ingenuity. Certainly the same was true of Mary and Joseph. They made the most of what they had on that blessed night that Christ was born. There was no place for them to stay so they found shelter with a group of farm animals. They didn't have a bed for their newborn infant so they laid Him in a feed trough. They didn't have clothes to keep Him warm so they wrapped Him in strips of cloth. My simple tagboard nativity scene was a symbol and a reminder that the richest people on earth are not the ones who have the most, but are the ones that required the least.

I returned to the dining room table to cut the construction paper into strips. I expertly glued them together to create a two-foot chain. It was not nearly long enough to encircle the tree even once. It would take weeks of "dumpster diving" to create a chain that would go around the tree several times as I had originally planned. It was getting late so I decided to attack the lack of tree ornaments tomorrow, hoping I would be inspired while I slept. I was determined to come up with Plan B by the following evening.

Much to my surprise, Plan B was waiting for me in my mailbox when I returned home from work the next day. It was a box wrapped in brown paper with my sister's address in the upper left hand corner. I quickly scooped up the box, unlocked the apartment door, and stepped inside. I immediately dropped my canvas bag of projects to grade, and ripped the paper off the box. Inside the shoebox were a dozen handmade Christmas ornaments with a note that read, "Merry Christmas! Love, Mary."

I carefully admired each decoration's simplistic beauty. The foundation of each ornament was sturdy, plastic netting. Needlepoint designs made of white, green, and red yarn covered the plastic. I picked up the ornaments one at a time, watching each one spin and twirl as if to show off its detailed designs, front and back. There were Santas, angels, stockings, and holly berries. How did she know? How did my sister know that I had splurged on a tree but had no money left to buy ornaments? I arranged those handmade ornaments on my tree with gratitude and care. Then I called my sister and thanked her for her timely and thoughtful gift.

Thirty years later, I still place those beautiful handmade ornaments on my tree with gratitude and care, and I am reminded of the Christmas I spent in a basement apartment on the wind swept plains of South Dakota. Even though I was poor in terms of financial wealth, I was rich in

Christmas spirit. I had learned an important lesson. Life is a magical mixture of being independent while still realizing the importance of relying on others. What a wonderful dichotomy.

Reflections
•The richest people on earth are not the ones who have the most, but are the ones that require the least.

•Life is a mixture of independence and interdependence. It is important to know that you can make it on your own, but it is also important to know that we all need other people. Independence develops your strength, but interdependence develops your depth.

•Make due with what you've got and develop a sense of gratitude.

•When you make a sacrifice to obtain your goals, you develop an appreciation for what you have obtained, and an appreciation for the skills and self-confidence you developed to reach those goals. Perhaps that is why that Christmas meant so much to me, because I had earned it.

Ornaments made by Mary

Life is a Puzzle

"Life is like a big puzzle that never really gets solved until the very end. All we can do is to try our best to gather the pieces, to make sense of the images we can form, and to hope that one day everything will make sense, and the picture formed will be far better than we ever expected it to be."
                                        -Author Unknown

Every since I was a young girl, I longed for my sister-in-law, Jane, to draw my name in our annual family Christmas drawing. Why? Because she gave people the most unique gifts. She seemed to know what you wanted for Christmas before you knew you wanted it, but perhaps it wasn't the gifts that were so unique as it was the giver.

Jane had married my brother Steve when they were both teenagers. While my older brother was a handsome young man, how he managed to marry a gorgeous, intelligent, thoughtful woman like Jane was beyond me. She had the uncanny ability to see beauty in everything, whether it was a shabby chic antique, the flowers in her garden, or the kindness of a friend.

Every year, as family members arrived at my parents' home for our Christmas celebration, I would greet them at the door with a warm hug and offer to take their gifts while they removed their coats and boots. My actions were meant to be a kind and thoughtful gesture, but I must admit I had another motive as well. As I gingerly carried bags and boxes to the basement where we opened our

77

gifts, I would carefully survey the nametags to see who had brought a present for me.

I was a young adult who had graduated from college when it finally happened. I greeted Steve, Jane, and their two boys at the door with heartfelt hugs. I gathered the gifts the boys were carrying and hauled them to the basement. As I added the boxes to the pile at the bottom of the stairs, I saw my name on a rectangular box about the size of a book. "To Pam, From Jane," the tag read.

"Sweet," I thought to myself. "This is going to be good."

I rushed up the stairs and found Mom in the kitchen.

"Mom, guess what? Jane had my name for Christmas!" I announced as I clapped my hands together like a giddy schoolgirl. Before she could respond, I was off to find my sister Mary in order to tell her the good news.

After we had stuffed ourselves with delicious food, cleared the tables, and washed the dishes, we all gathered in a big circle in the basement to open our gifts. Of course, there were the usual toys for the children, sweaters and candles for the ladies, wool socks and flannel shirts for the guys. Finally, it was my turn to open the gift from Jane. In a flurry of excitement, I ripped off the wrapping paper to find a one-of-a-kind, extraordinary nativity scene. Clearly, it was handmade from a light colored wood, which was possibly pine. The holy family, three wise men, shepherds and animals were abstract in design like pieces of modern sculpture. The most miraculous aspect of the design was the fact that each piece, each person or animal fit together like a puzzle inside the wooden frame of the manger. As I surveyed my gift, I couldn't surmise if it was a Christmas decoration or a work of art. I glanced up from my treasure to make eye contact with Jane.

"Thank you so much," I told her. "It's beautiful."

"I hoped you would like it," she said.

"Like it? I love it!" I gushed as I walked across the room to give her a quick hug.

Soon everyone had opened their gifts, and we began the clean up stage of the celebration. We bagged the torn wrapping paper, then loaded people, gifts, and leftovers into the cars.

Once everyone had left to journey back to their homes, I took the opportunity to admire the nativity scene with the time it deserved. Because of the abstract nature of the design, the race and age of the people was purposely unclear. The people could be of any race or any age you imagined. I thought to myself . . . wouldn't it be awesome if we could all see each other just as people and not in terms of skin color or how long you have lived on the planet? *What a wonderful world that would be.*

I delighted in the fact that the people and animals fit into the manger frame like a puzzle. Immediately, it reminded me of how Jane fit right into our family. Dad had always said there were no in-laws. Everyone was simply a family member.

The nativity scene reminded me of how each of us try to fit into different situations whether it is with our families, our friends, or coworkers.

Sometimes we need to smooth our rough edges or change our angles in order to fit in.

I sat quietly meditating for a few moments. Had Jane simply given me a beautiful, handmade nativity scene? Or had she given me a gift, which represented life itself? Each person and event in our lives fit together inside a frame created by God the Father's and the Holy Spirit's love with Jesus right in the middle of it all. Truly life is a puzzle. God had given us all the pieces, but it is up to us to fit them together.

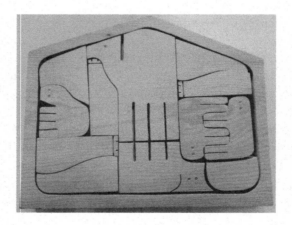

Reflections

•It is important to take the time to appreciate the people in your life.

•There is beauty in abstraction because people can create their own images and meanings.

•The people and events of your life fit together like a puzzle with God the Father and the Holy Spirit creating the important outer edges, which hold everything together, and Jesus as the heart of the puzzle.

It's About Time

"A man who dares to waste one hour of time has not discovered the value of life."

-Charles Darwin

"Chad was in a motorcycle accident," my mother's voice echoed from the telephone receiver. Chad was my seventeen-year-old nephew, my brother's son. "He's dead," she sobbed. She continued to explain the details of the crash, but all I heard was Chad is dead. *Chad is dead*, repeated in my mind.

Retelling the details of the accident had worked Mother into a state of hysteria so we ended our phone conversation. After I heard the click signaling she had hung up her phone, I sat frozen at the desk in my dorm room.

I had decided to take a year off from teaching to work on my master's degree in special education at the University of Northern Colorado in Greeley. I was living on campus in a dorm for the summer because it was the cheapest housing available. In the fall, I was planning on moving to a studio apartment near campus.

It was early morning at the time of the call. When I finally broke free from the trance I was in, I hung up the phone, looked down, and realized I was still in my pajamas. Maybe this was just a bad dream I thought to myself. That thought lasted only momentarily. I knew this was real. My beloved nephew was gone.

I had never lost anyone I loved before, so I wasn't sure how I was supposed to feel or react. I thought I should cry, but the tears wouldn't come. Little did I know I was in a state of denial and disbelief, which is the first stage in the grieving process. The tears would come later.

I knew I had to go back to Iowa to say goodbye to Chad and to grieve with my family. There was no question about it in my mind, but the question was how? I had a car, but not enough money for gas to drive that far. I barely had money for food each month. I showered, dressed, and prayed for a solution to my transportation problem.

My prayer was answered when the phone rang. It was my older sister, Barb. I explained to her that Mother had called and told me about Chad. Barb and her husband, Doug, owned a small plane. Doug was taking flying lessons, but hadn't earned his pilot's license yet. Barb and Doug had decided to hire a pilot to fly me home in their plane for the funeral. They would travel with me. All I had to do was to drive to a nearby, small airport and leave my car in the parking lot. I could do that. She explained the plane would arrive the following day around noon, and I thanked her repeatedly for her generous gesture.

As soon as I hung up the phone, I grabbed my backpack and headed to my classes. I stayed after each class to speak to the instructor, explaining I would be traveling to the Midwest to attend my nephew's funeral. The professors were very compassionate, expressing their thoughts of sympathy. One even hugged me.

I had one class left. It was Introduction to Emotional and Behavioral Handicaps. It met late in the afternoon. I dreaded the class not because of the time it met, but because of the professor who taught it. He was mean. Everyone working on a master's degree in special education knew about his reputation and tried to avoid taking his classes at all costs. During the summer sessions, the classes offered were limited. Unfortunately, he was the only instructor teaching the class during the summer, so I had no choice but to take it.

His class was basic "sit and get." We were required to read the textbook each evening then during class we would listen to him lecture on what we had read the night before. There were no discussions, no projects, no group work, and no thinking on your own or with anyone else. Occasionally, he would bark questions at us, and of course, he was quick to point out the stupidity of our answers. We were only allowed to speak to him during his office hours immediately after class. Of course, none of us were ever brave enough to do that.

I suffered through class, keeping my head down, and taking notes in the hope that if I avoided eye contact with the man, he wouldn't call on me. My strategy worked. After class, I was faced with the task of speaking to this tyrant one on one. I made my way to his office and reluctantly knocked on the door.

"Come in," he ordered in a gruff voice.

I slowly entered the small, cluttered room and took a seat in the chair across from his desk. He looked up from a stack of papers and peered at me over his thick, black rimmed glasses. There was no avoiding eye contact now.

I explained to him that my nephew had unexpectedly died in a motorcycle accident, and I would need to miss a few classes in order to travel to the Midwest to attend his funeral. By the time I finished speaking, my hands were sweating uncontrollably, a lump had developed in my throat as I choked out the words, and I was desperately fighting back the tears. I knew about his reputation and had experienced his wrath during class, but I had no idea how he was going to react to this situation. I simply hoped for the best.

"This is the most pathetic ploy to skip class that I have ever experienced," he sputtered. "For God's sake, he's your nephew, not an immediate family member! If you skip class, I have no choice but to give you an incomplete for the course."

I sat frozen in the chair with my mouth dropped open in disbelief. I knew the man was mean, but now I was questioning whether he was even human. Memories of Chad came flooding into my mind. I remember his parents, Steve and Jane, bringing him to our house when he was just a newborn. It was then that my mom gave me my first diaper-changing lesson on sweet, adorable Chad. When he was less than a year old, he could walk under our kitchen table. Because he was so small and so bow-legged, he looked like a cartoon cowboy who had ridden his horse far too long. Most teenagers were embarrassed about physical displays of emotion or affection, but not Chad. He still loved to hug everyone. His cousin, Michelle, was the same age and ironically she was the female version of Chad. "Two peas in a pod," my dad would say. They loved a game we called "Dog Pile." As soon as someone called out "Dog Pile," everyone jumped on the floor, wrestling each other, and creating a huge mountain of bodies. Chad and Michelle could always be found in one of two places on the pile. They were either on the bottom because they had called out the magic words and immediately jumped on the floor to create the pile, or they were on the top because they waited until everyone else had created the mound, then they jumped on the gigantic heap and triumphantly declared themselves the winners.

My fondest memory was the nickname Chad had created for my mother. Her first name was Shirley, but he always called her Grandma Squirrely. She truly was a unique lady who had a wonderful sense of humor, and a slightly twisted view of the world. The nickname fit her perfectly, and she loved it as much as she loved Chad.

As these memories tumbled from my brain, I felt a burning anger forming and rolling in the bottom of my gut. It welled up into my chest and eventually to my throat. Soon words were spewing from my mouth in a calm yet determined tone.

"First, let me say that I love my nephew like a brother. You have no right to tell me what the 'value' of my relationship with him was, or whether he is worthy of my attendance at his funeral," I began. "You can do to me whatever you want, but I am going to his funeral. When I return, I will be sitting in your class. Even if you give me an incomplete, I have the right to audit the course." Then I stood up, walked out, and shut the door behind me before he could speak. My legs were shaking so much that I could hardly walk down the stairs, so I grabbed the handrail to steady myself. I had never spoken that way to anyone in a position of authority, but I didn't regret my actions. In fact, I was glad I did it.

I returned to my dorm room to eat the evening meal and to pack. I tumbled into bed that night emotionally exhausted from the day's events. I woke the next morning to the irritating sound of my alarm clock. Once again I hoped I was waking up from a bad dream, but when I surveyed the room and saw my packed suitcase, I knew it was real.

I leisurely showered, dressed, ate breakfast, grabbed my suitcase, and drove to the airport outside of town. The airport was exactly what I expected. It consisted of a windsock, one runway, and a large metal building.

The small plane landed, and my sister and her husband emerged from the aircraft. They met me inside the building at the bench where I had been patiently waiting. I grabbed Barb, hugging her so hard that I thought her eyes would pop out of her head. As we embraced, we both began to cry, sobbing as if we were one person.

"Come on, girls. Let's go," her husband instructed us as he beckoned toward the runway. He grabbed my suitcase, and we walked to the plane.

Soon, we were in the air with Doug sitting up front with the pilot. Barb and I sat in the back gazing out of the windows, and admiring the patchwork quilt created by the fields of corn, soybeans, and alfalfa. My mind began to wander to thoughts of Chad.

"Chad never met a stranger," my dad would say. Because Chad was so friendly, people were naturally attracted to him. He could easily join any conversation. He was clever, witty, and fun. I wondered how we would all survive without his big bear hugs, impromptu jokes, the twinkle in his eyes when he was up to no good, and his incredible, infectious laugh. There was a gaping hole left in the fabric of our family. Who would take his little brother, Brandon, under their wing? Who would tease the younger cousins? Who would hunt with Steve and Dad? Who would be the hero we all cheered for during football games? No one could replace Chad. How were we going to live without our sweet, sweet boy?

A patch of turbulence interrupted my thoughts. Suddenly, Barb and I were being tossed about like lettuce leaves in a salad bowl. My wise, older sister reached beneath our seats to retrieve two barf bags. She handed one to me just in the nick of time, and I immediately deposited my breakfast in the small, paper pouch. I don't know if my physical illness was being caused by the rollercoaster effect the turbulence had on my stomach or by my emotional distress caused by the realization that I would never see Chad again. Perhaps, it was a little of both. I did find it rather ironic that the turbulence seemed to be a symbol for the rough patch in life that our family was about to face. Just as Barb was looking out for me in the plane, we would all get through this crisis, this "turbulence" together.

We landed, picked up Barb and Doug's car, and drove to my parents' home. Even though I longed for a calm, peaceful environment, I knew I would encounter a new kind of "turbulence," a house full of well meaning, kind-hearted family members and friends.

Mom and Dad greeted us at the door with long embraces. We didn't speak. Words didn't seem necessary. "Food is love" is a famous old saying, and by the looks of our kitchen, I would say our family was well loved. Casserole dishes, salads, and desserts covered every inch of counter space. Just as the food had invaded the kitchen, every room in the house was occupied with people. Although I couldn't hear exact words, a mild buzz from conversations filled the house.

I deposited my suitcase in the back bedroom then circulated through the crowd in each room, sharing hugs and memories of Chad as a way to process the shocking hand life had dealt us.

After several hours, most people left to return to their own homes, leaving us to finally face our grief alone. We hadn't eaten lunch but merely snacked on sandwiches and finger foods throughout the afternoon. Mom asked us if we were hungry. We responded with intense and vehement noes. After helping tidy up the house, my sisters gathered their families and went home. Mom, Dad, and I decided to travel to Steve and Jane's (Chad's parents) home in the nearby town of Swea City.

When we walked into their house, we were greeted by the same scenario we had just left. The house was filled with wall-to-wall people and bursting at the seams with food.

We found Steve and Jane in the kitchen surrounded by their friends. Instinctively, we went to hug them. My sister-in-law, Jane, has always been a goddess to me. She was beautiful, intelligent, thoughtful, loving, and witty. Certainly, Chad had inherited much of his personality from her. On this particular evening, Jane's gorgeous face had been transformed. Her eyes were puffy and red. Her cheeks were tear stained, and her heart-warming smile was gone. Clearly, there was nothing beautiful about grief.

Steve grabbed me for a bear hug, pounding me twice on the back as if it were Morse code for two important words, thank you. Thank you for coming. Thank you for loving Chad. Thank you for loving me. Once again, no words were necessary.

While Chad had inherited much of his personality from his mom, he inherited his physical features from his dad. He had Steve's dark hair, brown eyes, physical stature, and his playful, impish grin. He did inherit an important personality trait from his father. He was mischievous, not naughty, because there is a difference. Chad didn't break rules on purpose. Instead, he was very curious and fun-loving. Often the rules were broken on the way to achieving laughter and having a good time. As a young boy, he was a free spirit. It was amazing what Chad could think of to do for fun. He was always running, jumping, climbing, and covered in dirt. He lived life at a speed, which I refer to as "Mach ten with your hair on fire." This undaunted creature was an only child for a very long time, when suddenly his brother, Brandon, entered the picture and changed Chad's life on many different levels. Much to Brandon's dismay, Chad became the responsible, protective, older brother. Brandon had inherited his father's mischievous nature as well. But little did he know all the wonderful adventures and fun activities he thought of, Chad had already conceived in his beady brain and had actually carried them out. Hoping to save Brandon from the heartaches, spankings, bumps and bruises he had experienced, Chad tried to stop his younger brother from making some of the same mistakes he had made. At times it must have seemed like a full time job for Chad because Brandon was smart, clever, and very quick. Despite Chad's daily efforts to protect his brother, Brandon continually found ways to get into trouble. Keep in mind the trouble wasn't anything big, just a young boy's search for adventure and fun. Life without Chad was going to be hard for all of us, but particularly for Brandon.

I searched the house for Brandon, and finally found him in the basement sitting on a couch with several adults. Usually, he would have been running outside or playing with his toys, but not tonight. He was content to take turns sitting on the laps of friends and relatives and snuggling. Over the next few days we would all need some extra love, but especially Brandon.

For years I have tried to remember the day of Chad's funeral, but I can't. It is simply a blur. Perhaps, I purposely erased those images and feelings in order to avoid the excruciating pain. I must admit there is one thing I do remember and that was the look on the faces of the kids who went to school with Chad. His high school had less than two hundred students so everybody hung out together. Granted, it wasn't a perfect situation. Even in a small high school, there were still cliques. There were the jocks, the cheerleaders, and the nerds, but they managed to exist together and were friends. On the day of the funeral, it wasn't just the kids from Chad's class who came to the church to say goodbye; it was the entire student body. It was hard to see them hugging one another, their bodies shaking as they sobbed in each other's arms. It didn't seem fair that people at such a young age had to endure such deep pain. But as the year progressed, they found ways to express their grief and sorrow, ways that helped them to heal individually and as a group. The football team wore black armbands that season to honor their lost player. Chad was remembered at many school events like homecoming, the prom, and graduation. Even though Chad couldn't physically be with his friends, they made sure he was always with them in spirit.

One thing I quickly learned about grief is that you must work your way through the stages. Remaining in a stage of grief can be dangerous.

The only way to work through grief is through action. You must go on living, and you must realize that the person you lost would want it that way. Just as Chad's friends continued their lives but also remembered him, I needed to continue my life, taking a little piece of him with me.

I returned to Greeley to continue my coursework. It actually felt good to return to my classes and to continue to study what I loved. Of course, there was the dreaded professor who had threatened to flunk me if I missed any of his classes, but I was true to my word. I went to his class. I sat in my assigned seat ready for the "sit and get." Much to my surprise, on my first day back he asked me to stay after class. *I am in for it now.* I thought to myself.

As my classmates exited the room, I felt a huge knot forming in the pit of my stomach. I slung my backpack over my shoulder and headed to the front of the room to speak with my instructor.

"Ms. Wegner, I was wrong," he began. Wow! That took me off guard. I knew he would never say he was sorry or would never apologize, but just to hear him say he was wrong was shocking.

"You can read the chapters you missed and write summaries for them. If you complete those tasks, you can continue in this class, and I won't give you an incomplete," he continued.

"Thank you. I appreciate your understanding," I responded. Then I walked out of the classroom in a state of total disbelief. I knew this situation wasn't going to melt that angry professor's heart. Let's get serious. That only happens on TV shows and in movies. But perhaps it did make his icy heart thaw just a little, not because of a short conversation with a graduate student, but because a loving aunt dared to show her emotions, dared to show her love for a beloved nephew, and dared to show she was human.

The professor's class was still "sit and get" for the remainder of summer, but he seemed to soften a little and was less likely to embarrass us in front of the class. Many of us dared to raise our hands and wanted to be called on. I actually learned information and strategies in the class and eventually earned a "B" instead of an incomplete.

Fall semester arrived, and I moved to my studio apartment off campus. I took a weekend job at a residential facility for mentally disabled adults. This was an incredible experience. I was able to teach the residents life skills such as grocery shopping, budgeting, cooking, cleaning, and recreation. After all life can't be all work and no play. The residents became my friends. I gained valuable experience for my career, and I had an income.

When Christmas rolled around, I had money to pay for the gas to drive back to Iowa. Unfortunately, I didn't have much money for gifts. It was our first Christmas without Chad, so I wanted to give everyone something that would continue our healing process. As I thought back over the events shortly after Chad's death, I realized that each time I was faced with grief and sorrow, I replaced those emotions with joy and happiness just by thinking about the memories I had of my nephew. It happened when Mom called to tell me Chad was gone. It happened when I confronted my professor. It happened on the plane ride home. It happened in my parents home, in my brother's home, and at the funeral. In the months that followed, I realized that what I loved the most about my relationship with Chad was the time we spent together. Sharing time together is how memories are made. I also realized what I would miss the most about Chad was the time we wouldn't be able to spend together. I would never see him graduate from high school, get married, have a career, or become a parent. It made me realize that our lives are all about time and how we spend it. How ironic that time was something I loved and hated. It was a huge lesson to learn that time needed to be cherished. None of us know when our time here on earth will end. How could any of us have known that Chad's time would be so short, only seventeen years? I came to the conclusion that I wanted my gift to represent time. I brainstormed ideas . . . watches, clocks, a calendar. That was it! I would create a family calendar.

This was before digital photography and the Internet. We did have computers but mainly for word processing. I created a calendar in the campus computer lab. Then I begged my mom to send me photographs of weddings, birthdays, anniversaries, kids, and family gatherings. I swore on my life I would bring the photos home with me at Christmas. She thought it was a great way to insure that I came home for the holidays, so she agreed to help me.

I took my calendar pages, photographs, and ideas to a copy/print shop. I created a collage of each family member for every month of the year, paying close attention to the one highlighting Chad. I added birthdays and anniversaries, copied the pages, and connected the pages with a plastic, spiral binding. The photos were copied in black and white, but I didn't care. I thought it was beautiful. It was an "all nighter" at the print shop. Because I did all the work myself and only used their machines, I kept the cost to a minimum. I wrapped the calendars with pride, and I was so excited to see each family member's reaction to my homemade gift.

Normally, you would think the wiser, older aunt would be the one to teach the nephew a lesson, but in reality, the opposite was true. My nephew Chad taught me one of the greatest, lasting lessons that I will ever learn. He taught me the meaning of life . . . it is all about time. Chad taught me how precious time is. In less than a second Chad's time on earth was taken away. Our lives are measured in time . . . seconds, minutes, hours, weeks, and years, but how time passes is not what is truly important. What is truly important is how we chose to spend it.

Reflections
•Life is all about time and how you spend it.
•Time should be cherished. You never know when your time here on earth will end.
•The sorrow of grief can be replaced by the joy and happiness contained in memories. You can make a conscious effort to control those emotions and move through the stages of grief.

•Life is not only about time, but it is also about timing. My interaction with my professor taught me about when it was the right time to learn how to stand up for myself, my values, and my beliefs. Perhaps, it was also the right time for my instructor to learn a life lesson as well.

Chad
Wegner

A Colorado Christmas

"The measure of intelligence is the ability to change."

-Albert Einstein

As a flatlander who had transplanted herself to the Rocky Mountains, I found I had many adjustments to make. But I gladly made sacrifices and lifestyle changes in order to call the gorgeous state of Colorado my home.

First, there was the altitude to contend with. My lungs were accustomed to the oxygen density found at sea level. I quickly learned the Rocky Mountain high John Denver so beautifully sang about was probably caused by oxygen deprivation. As we all know, the higher the altitude, the less dense the atmosphere. This explained why I was gasping for air after light physical activity. Fortunately, after a few months, my lungs acclimated to the new environment.

Second, the weather in the Rocky Mountains is a true anomaly. Coloradans often say that if you don't like the weather, just wait a few minutes, and it will change. This is not a myth. I repeat. This is not a myth. It is true. A day can start at sixty or seventy degrees with not a cloud in the sky. In a matter of minutes, clouds roll in, the temperature drops, and you find yourself in a snowstorm. People in Colorado dress in layers due to these uncertain weather conditions. A light jacket or sweatshirt can be worn over a short-sleeved shirt.

When it is warm, you can remove the jacket or sweatshirt and tie it around your waist. When it is cold, you snuggle into that sweatshirt and pop up the hood as added protection against the wicked weather elements.

I quickly learned a backpack is not just a fashion accessory, which increases your "cool factor." It is actually a survival necessity. Over the years, I learned to include these items in my backpack: a filled water bottle, snacks, flashlight, gloves, stocking hat, rain poncho, and an extra jacket. I must admit I have learned to love the unpredictable weather, and I have found it has also taught me many lessons including to be prepared for anything Mother Nature may throw my way.

Next, living in the West has taught me to value water. In the Midwest, water was everywhere, under the ground, in rivers and lakes, and in the air in the form of humidity. In Colorado, every drop of this precious liquid is valued as if it were gold. People manipulate it by building dams to create reservoirs. They control its flow with irrigation ditches. At one time, it was against the law to collect rainwater in the state of Colorado. Is that crazy, or what? On a personal level, I found I needed to drink large quantities of water to maintain my health in such an arid climate.

As the years passed, I found myself to be quite the chameleon in that I easily adapted to my new surroundings, but one thing I never expected to be different was Christmas.

When I was growing up in Iowa, we always had an artificial, silver tree made out of aluminum. It was stored in a box in the guest bedroom. We ate oyster stew on Christmas Eve, even though none of us liked it. When we were little, Santa Claus actually came to our home on Christmas Eve. We sat on his lap and hugged his neck. He would reach into his bag and pull out our Christmas gifts. It was a joyous event except for one sad part. My sister's husband, Ron, was never able to meet dear, old Saint Nick. Strangely enough, Ron was always in the bathroom when Santa arrived. Santa never came to our home in the middle of the night because we had something else to do at that time. We all went to midnight mass. On Christmas Day, approximately thirty people would gather at my parents' home for a giant feast, which was served at twelve o'clock sharp. After the delicious meal of roasted turkey with all of the fixings, we would gather in a circle with our gifts situated in front of us. We would take turns opening our gifts starting with the youngest person and ending with the oldest. In this manner, we could see what everyone had received, and we could thank people right on the spot. It was all very organized and civilized.

The first Christmas in Colorado was something of a culture shock. My husband, Greg, and I traveled to the western slope of the state to spend the holidays with his family, and we stayed at his mother's home.

When Christmas morning arrived, Greg woke me from my slumber by shaking my shoulder. "Wake up. It's Christmas!" he instructed me.

I glanced out of the bedroom window. "No way! It's night. It's still dark outside!" I told him.

"Come on! Get out of bed!" he responded as he turned on the ceiling light, which allowed me to see my frightening reflection in the window. Two white lines of dried drool marked the outer corners of my mouth. These were matched by two crusty globs of who knows what in the corners of my eyes. My short, curly hair looked like I had spent the night in a wind tunnel at a NASA test facility. On top of that, my mouth was dry, and my breath smelled like dog food.

"You have got to be kidding me," I muttered. "Can I at least brush my teeth?" I asked.

"No, put this on," he ordered as he threw me my fuzzy robe. "We're going to open our gifts."

I donned my robe, slipped on a pair of socks, and shuffled to the living room in a zombie-like trance. Greg's mom, Inez, was seated in a cushioned chair wearing a velvet bathrobe. With her hair brushed and her glasses on, she was surrounded by beautifully wrapped boxes adorned with ribbons and bows. She looked like an elegant Christmas queen.

How did she do that? I said to myself as I thought of my peasant-like appearance.

Greg motioned for me to sit in the comfy chair between his mom and him. It was just the three of us surrounded by mounds of packages.

Inez greeted me with a joyful "Merry Christmas," and I echoed the holiday greeting back to her.

"Let's start!" Greg bellowed, and in an instant the sound of ripping wrapping paper filled the room. Paper, ribbon, and bows soared through the air as if a tornado from the Midwest had arrived. I sat frozen in my chair, as if in shock from the sight before me. In a matter of minutes, Greg and his mom had opened their gifts and were already in the kitchen beginning to make breakfast.

Somehow, I managed to break free from the trance I was in and realized I was still holding the first package I had been given. I proceeded to unwrap the gift and admire it. When I looked around the room to thank someone, I realized I was the only one there. I continued to open the rest of my gifts. When my task was complete, I was unsure what to do next. There was no one around to thank and in the flurry of activity, I had no idea what Greg and his mom had received as gifts. After surveying the situation, I decided the correct plan of action was to join Greg and Inez in the kitchen to help with the preparation of breakfast.

As the years progressed, Greg and I learned about the power of compromise, not only about our Christmas traditions but about life in general. Compromise is not only a great way for everyone to be a winner, but also to have the best of multiple situations.

Greg is an avid outdoorsman who likes to fish and hunt. So the interior of our home is filled with large, taxidermied fish and an assortment of deer antlers. The outside of our home is decorated with wooden forest creatures including a black bear and a gray raccoon. As part of our compromise agreement, when Christmas arrives each year, I add my creative touches. The fish and the forest creatures proudly display their Christmas spirits by wearing fuzzy Santa hats, and the deer antlers mysteriously become intertwined with colorful, festive Christmas lights. Our Christmas stockings, which are shaped like cowboy boots, add a unique Colorado flare to the fireplace mantle.

As for Christmas Day, we have created our own traditions by combining a little from each of our families. We awake early at sunrise on Christmas morning to open our gifts, but we open them one person at a time in age order.

Perhaps, our Christmas compromises and my adaption to a new state and environment are just simple symbols representing a much larger idea. It is the idea that Jesus Christ, our Lord and Savior, came from heaven to earth to live as a common person rather than a deity. That truly is the ultimate example of adaption and melding of two environments . . . heaven and earth.

Reflections
•We all compromise and adapt as a matter of survival. Sometimes we aren't even aware of this phenomenon.
•Compromise can be a win/win situation, offering the best of multiple solutions.
•Like any parent, God gives us positive examples of how we should live our lives, like the examples of adaption, compromise, and generosity He gave us through sending His son to live in our world.

Hope

The best way to not feel hopeless is to get up and do something. Don't wait for good things to happen. If you go out and make good things happen, you will fill the world and yourself with hope.
-Barack Obama

Greg and I had been married a little over a year when I was diagnosed with severe endometriosis, which affected our ability to conceive a child. For several years, we worked with an infertility specialist in Denver and a well-respected obstetrician/ gynecologist in Colorado Springs. The situation was not only a surprise but also ironic. We were both educators who had devoted our lives to helping children learn, grow, and reach their potentials, yet we seemed to be unable to have children ourselves.

This realization was emotionally painful. If that wasn't enough, my life was filled with physical pain as well. Every day I struggled to walk without being bent over in pain. I persevered and became quite the skilled actress, covering up the pain with my positive attitude and wacky sense of humor.

Twice a year, usually during summer and winter breaks from school, I would have surgeries to remove large ovarian cysts, and to laser off the endometrial tissue that stuck my abdominal organs together like glue. At one point, I suggested to my obstetrician/gynecologist that she should insert a zipper across my abdomen, so she could unzip it, work her magic, and zip it back up. She found no humor in this suggestion.

My other suggestions were more serious in nature but were met with the same disregard. I often suggested that she have a couple of days during each month set aside for women who weren't pregnant, women who were facing infertility issues or simply wanted an annual checkup. My rational for this was that it was emotionally draining for me to sit in the waiting room filled with pregnant women whose protruding bellies were an "in your face" reminder that I would never experience the miracle of conceiving a child. Certainly, I wasn't the only one who felt this way.

"It's too much of a scheduling nightmare," was the doctor's standard response.

"Could you at least get a variety of reading material in the waiting area?" I would counter. "It's difficult to sit out there surrounded by parenting magazines when I doubt I am ever going to be a parent. Could you add some *People* magazines or a few copies of *Good Housekeeping*? *Time*? *Field and Stream*? Anything?"

"I'll check into it," she would reply. Never happened.

What did happen during each appointment was the summary of the handy-dandy stages of endometriosis chart. The chart was approximately four inches wide and about two feet long when "unfurled." It was folded like an accordion, and each fold represented a stage of the disease with the most severe stage at the very end.

"As you know, there are various levels of endometriosis," she would start as she pointed to the beginning of the chart. "Your case is over here," she would continue as she waved her hand in the air at the end of the chart. "It's off the chart. It's the worst case I have experienced in my entire medical career. My recommendation is that you have a hysterectomy."

This scenario was replayed twice a year for several years. Each time, I would decline the offer of having a hysterectomy, stating that I wanted to continue to work with my infertility doctor with the hope of having a child.

Finally, during one of these predictable appointments, the physician added, " I don't know how much more of this your body can take."

The room went silent. I knew she was right. I didn't know how much more of the pain, or the physical damage the disease was doing to my body, that I could take. I knew in my heart that no matter how many infertility drugs I took, no matter how many procedures I underwent, I was never going to have a baby.

I hung my head in defeat and in a loud voice, I announced, "Okay, I'll do it. I'll have the hysterectomy."

"Are you sure?" the doctor asked in disbelief. "Do you want to go home and discuss this with your husband?"

"No," I answered. "We've discussed this many times over the years, and he always tells me that it is my body and my decision." I rose to exit the room.

"You won't regret this. You will feel so much better," she assured me as she gave me a hug.

As I walked down the hall to the front desk to schedule the surgery, I felt like I already regretted the decision. I had just given up any chance of ever having a child. Once those body parts were removed, there was no going back. I would never know what it feels like to have another human being grow inside my body or feel that child move in my abdomen. I would never hold our newborn baby in my arms or watch our offspring grown into an adult. I would never be a parent. I would never be a mom.

All of my hope was gone. All that was left was nothingness. The chart my doctor had shared with me so many times over the years was the perfect symbol of this. Each time she waved her hand in the air at the end of the chart, there was nothing there. The end of the chart was the end of my hope. With no hope left, I felt as if I had fallen into a bottomless hole with nothing to stop my fall. The abyss was dark and frightening. No matter how I tried to grab at the sides of the hole, my actions were in vain, and the free-fall continued. I knew the only way to stop the fall was to find hope again. It seemed as elusive as the air we breathe and just as necessary for survival. Where could I find hope? The answer came to me in a logical place . . . church.

I was in church on a Sunday morning a couple of weeks before my scheduled hysterectomy. Greg was on a summer fishing trip in Canada with a group of his buddies, so I was enjoying the worship service without him. We had come to the part of mass when each person silently offers up his or her individual needs and intentions. I offered up all of my worries regarding not being able to have a family. I closed my eyes envisioning myself holding a gigantic, dark, rumbling thundercloud in my arms. I was wrestling the storm in an effort to get it under control, when another set of hands reached out to take it from me. Suddenly, it was gone from my grasp and gone from my sight. I opened my eyes with a sense of calmness and confidence. I felt at peace.

Music filled the interior of the church, and the congregation began singing the next hymn "Here I Am, Lord." With my worries gone, I felt like I could belt out a song of praise with gusto, passion, and a little extra zip in my voice. When we began to sing the chorus, something strange happened. The words echoed inside the church and inside my brain.

Here I am, Lord.

Is it I, Lord?

I have heard you calling in the night.

I will go, Lord.

If you lead me.

I will hold your people in my heart.

I felt a tingling sensation all over my body. I looked down at my arms. Sure enough, there were goosebumps. I knew at that moment what God was calling Greg and I to do. We weren't supposed to create another human being. We were supposed to care for a child of God who already existed. Just as the song implied, I was asking God, "Is it I, Lord? Have you called me to do your will? Here I am, Lord. I will go where you lead me. I won't hold our biological child in my arms, but I will hold one of your children, one of your people in my arms."

I sat down, closed my eyes, and let this revelation sink in. Immediately, a vision appeared. A giant ball of light replaced the thunderstorm I had previously been holding in my outstretched arms. What was the giant ball of light representing? It was hope. My free-fall was over. I had found hope.

The next eighteen months were a whirlwind of activities. The surgery was completed. We found the Hand in Hand Adoption Agency to help us begin the adoption process. There were parenting classes to take, documents to collect, paperwork to fill out, interviews by social workers, and meetings with our case manager. I felt like this was our version of labor in the birthing process because this was the time when all the hard work took place. Finally, we were found worthy to be parents. There was nothing left to do but wait to be matched with a child in the Philippines, the country God had directed us to choose.

After months of waiting, the match was made and the dossier of our child arrived at the adoption agency's office. Butterflies were fluttering in my stomach, as we sat across the desk from our case manager. Carefully she placed the file folder that contained all the information about our child in front of us. Eagerly we opened the folder, and were greeted by the face of our one-year old daughter in the form of a photograph. As expected, she had dark hair, brown eyes, and beautiful tan skin. What we didn't expect was the mischievous twinkle in her eyes. I held the photograph close to my heart as we read through the documents contained in the folder. Her name was Arcelie, which was a common name in the Philippines. Due to her friendly, outgoing personality, Arcelie's crib had been placed near the front door of the house, which had been converted into an orphanage, so she could greet everyone who entered. Recently, she had learned to escape from her crib, so she was being moved to an orphanage in the countryside where older children lived. Clearly, our little Arcelie was a livewire.

Now, it was our turn to send a photograph of ourselves to her. Along with the photograph, we sent a small ragdoll for Arcelie to hold and snuggle, until we could arrive to hold and snuggle our little girl.

We were scheduled to meet our daughter at the orphanage in the Philippines on December 11th, which was two months away. The additional waiting time was actually a blessing because there were many tasks to complete. We prepared Arcelie's room, attended baby showers, organized our travel documents, collected donations for the orphanages (one in Manila and one in the countryside), purchased gifts for the caregivers at the orphanages, and bought our airline tickets.

Before we knew it, we were waving down a cab outside the airport in Manila. As we drove through the crowded streets, I sensed an exciting energy about the city. For one thing, cars traveled through the streets bumper to bumper, almost as if they were connected into one mass of metal. There were very few traffic lights at the intersections. Drivers had an innate sense of when it was their turn to proceed. Everyone constantly honked the cars' horns. When I asked our driver about this phenomenon, he politely explained, "They honk the horns to tell the other drivers where they are." It seemed like organized chaos to me, but to the people who lived in Manila, it made perfect sense. I think that is what happens when you travel to a new place. You begin to see the differences and similarities between where you are from and where you have traveled to. Since it was the Christmas season, I began thinking of how it was for Joseph and Mary to travel from their home to Bethlehem for the census.

It was then that I began to realize there were many similarities between our family and the Holy Family. Like Mary and Joseph, we had left our home, traveled many miles to an unknown place to meet our child. The children in both cases had existed in other places before being united with their adopted parents. Jesus had existed in heaven, while Arcelie existed in the Philippines. But that's where the similarities ended. While Joseph and Mary waited in a stable for their child to arrive, we were going to wait at the Holiday Inn.

After breakfast the next morning, we situated ourselves in two comfortable chairs in the Holiday Inn's lobby to wait for our assigned social worker, Beth. We had no idea what she looked like, so we merely waited for her to approach us.

Beth would take us to meet our daughter. She would also be spending the week with our new family, showing us the sights, allowing us to soak in the culture, but mainly to observe our interactions with Arcelie. Once again, we would be under the microscope, trying to prove we were fit to be parents.

Suddenly, a beautiful Filipino woman in her late thirties appeared before us.

"Are you Greg and Pam?" she asked in a soft voice that barely registered above a whisper.

"Yes, you must be Beth," Greg answered as we both rose from the chairs to shake Beth's hand.

"You must be very excited," Beth said as she led us to a car waiting at the front of the hotel.

"That is an understatement," I shared as Greg and I slid into the back seat of the sedan.

Beth opened the door on the passenger side and popped inside the vehicle. Once inside, she introduced us to the driver, who happened to be her cousin. He was a kind and friendly man who was about her age. When Beth and her cousin talked to each other on our journey to the orphanage, they spoke in Tagalog, the native language of the Philippines. When they talked to us, they spoke in English. Through our research, we had learned that most Filipinos were bilingual, speaking Tagalog, a native language with many dialects, and English. We found this to be intriguing, and were hoping to pick up a few words in Tagalog that we could incorporate with our interactions with Arcelie.

Beth and her cousin were very friendly and outgoing, and we felt at ease with them immediately. They were excellent tour guides who were eager to share with us the country and traditions they loved. They delighted in telling us about the delicious Filipino food, including a variety of fresh fruits and vegetables, which could be purchased at any of the produce stands that lined the city streets and rural roads.

Traveling through the rough, narrow streets of Manila, we sensed that the Christmas spirit was alive and thriving in this busy city. Christmas tree lots were on every street corner. Since evergreen trees are not native in a tropical climate, the lots were filled with leafless, deciduous trees that were spray painted hot pink, lime green, vibrant yellow, and florescent orange.

Star-shaped lanterns of every imaginable size and color adorned the store windows and street lampposts. Our driver proudly explained that these traditional Filipino lanterns were called paroles and symbolized the star, which shone so brightly over Bethlehem on the night Christ was born.

I asked Beth about the unusual vehicles that traversed the busy streets. She explained these were jeepneys, which were a cross between a jeep and a bus. They were the most common form of public transportation in the urban areas of the Philippines. These forms of transportation were covered but had open tailgate areas where people would climb in, deposit coins in the fee box, and find a place to sit on the side benches.

Jeepneys were as unique as each individual owner. It was as if there was an underlying competition taking place to see which jeepney had the most radical, creative, almost outlandish artwork painted on the exterior. The experience of watching the jeepneys on the streets was like being in an outdoor museum where the masterpieces actually appealed to spectators through sight, sound, and motion. These colorful vehicles zigzagged through the traffic, stopping periodically to load and unload passengers. The well-known melodies, which blasted into the atmosphere from their horns, were as unique as the artwork that adorned the exteriors. Sounds of conversations, laughter, and music exploded from the glassless windows, and the open tailgate areas.

Jeepneys seemed to be an expression of fun, but also at this time of year, they were an expression of Christmas. They were decorated with paroles (star lanterns), tinsel garland, ornaments, and colorful strings of Christmas lights, which were probably powered by the vehicles' batteries.

While jeepneys were moving pieces of artwork, the churches in the city were stationary forms of art. The classic arches, bell towers, and stained glass windows were breathtaking. Star lanterns, garlands, and poinsettias enhanced the already stunning architecture and gave each house of worship a bit of Christmas flare.

Truly, Christmas in the Philippines was a religious experience, not a commercial one. There were no Santas, reindeer, or elves. Instead, homes and businesses proudly displayed beautiful, unique nativity scenes. The inhabitants of the city were recreating the hope felt by the ancient people as they waited for Christ's birth.

It was no accident that the city of Manila was filled with the Christmas spirit as well as a sense of hope. It didn't just happen. People made it happen through their actions. They decorated their homes and businesses (and even jeepneys). They sang the Christmas carols that permeated the air. They delighted in preparing the traditional Christmas foods. They made a conscious effort to think about the birth of Jesus, and it's eternal implications of hope.

Just as the people of Manila had created hope through their actions, Greg and I had created our hope of having a family through our actions. We had gone through the adoption process with the help of the Hand in Hand Agency. We had taken the parenting classes, attended the meetings, completed the interviews, filled out the paperwork, and paid the fees. Then we had traveled halfway around the world with the hope of meeting our daughter and becoming a family. Ironically, this was all happening in a city of hope in the season of hope.

For our convenience, Arcelie had been moved from the orphanage in the countryside back to the orphanage in Manila where she had originally lived. As we pulled up in front of the orphanage, which was merely a small white house on a residential street, my palms began to sweat, and it wasn't from the heat and humidity. I was nervous. *What if our little girl was afraid of us? After all, we were complete strangers. What if she cried? What if I didn't know how to take care of her?*

Stop! This is nonsense. I told myself. *Just enjoy the moment.*

I drew strength from Greg by holding his hand as we walked through the door of that small, white house. There she was in a crib right inside the door, just as the papers in the dossier had explained. She immediately reached out her arms to me as if begging me to save her from the confinement of her crib. This time my arms weren't holding a dark thunderstorm of worry or a glowing orb representing hope. This time my arms were holding our daughter for the very first time. I held her close, pressing her cheek against mine as a way to make sure she was real and not a figment of my imagination. Greg hugged us both, kissing her sweet, little forehead. I will cherish that moment for as long as I live, and I will take it with me to the afterlife. It was the moment we became a family. It was a moment created by our actions, and our faith. We had created our own hope.

Reflections

•Hope gives us something to look forward to. It is as necessary as the air we breathe or the food we eat.
•Hope isn't always something that spontaneously happens. It can be created through our actions.
•Sometimes God's plan for us is different than the plan we have for ourselves. Trust in God's plan.
•Jesus Christ, our Lord and Savior, is the ultimate hope. He offers us redemption from our sins and eternal life.

Arcelie 1996

Sierra Arcelie
Pottorff 2013

116

I Did It!

"I can't do it," never yet accomplished anything.
"I will try," has performed wonders.

-George P. Burnham

Our preschool-aged daughter, Sierra, had been trying to put on her shoes by herself for several weeks. On this particular day, she was finally successful, and her excitement spilled out in these three important words, "I did it!" It was the first complete sentence she ever spoke. Those three simple words conveyed so much in terms of independence, pride, and a sense of accomplishment.

My husband, Greg, and I had tried to encourage our daughter's independence. When we first met Sierra, she was fourteen months old and living in a small house, which served as an orphanage for a dozen children in the city of Manila in the Philippines. It was clear she had been designated as the official greeter at the orphanage because her crib was adjacent to the front door.

It was naptime for the children on the day we arrived. When we opened the front door of the home, Sierra's head popped up from her crib. Immediately, she stood up, reaching out her arms for me to pick her up.

We had been sent a few photographs of her, which were priceless as we waited for Sierra's adoption to be completed. From the photos, I knew this darling little girl was our daughter, so I didn't hesitate in hoisting her out of the crib. I squeezed her tightly just to make sure she was real. She, on the other hand, was too busy looking around the room to hug me back. As soon as she saw Greg, she stretched her arms out to him as if to say, "Take me, take me." It was at that moment we knew Sierra was very independent. We had never met her before, but that didn't stop her from reaching out to us. We basically were her ticket out of the crib and out of the orphanage, so she could explore the world around her.

We continued to see her independent spirit on our scheduled outings with our social worker. As we visited several tourist attractions in Manila and the surrounding countryside, Sierra continued to greet people with baby talk and friendly waves. Obviously, she charmed everyone she met. Many people commented on how friendly she was. We thought this was amazing for a little girl who rarely went outside the walls of the small orphanage.

That fateful day when we first met Sierra was in early December. In fact, we have always believed that she was a very special Christmas gift sent to us from God. We have also felt very lucky we were able to experience Christmas in the Philippines. There is nothing else like it. The fabulous decorations, including lanterns called paroles, lined the streets. Lights and ornaments covered the buildings inside and out. The food was fantastic and included fresh fruits, as well as candies and cookies, to celebrate the blessed holiday.

When the holiday season arrived the following year, I wondered how our simple Colorado

Christmas could match the elegance and excitement of a Filipino Christmas.

It was the first Saturday in December. Greg had to supervise an activity at the middle school where he worked, so Sierra and I were home together for the day. Snow was falling, lightly covering the ground and the ponderosa pine trees, which surrounded our home.

The night before, Greg and I had brought our artificial Christmas tree up from the basement storage room and assembled it in front of the huge picture window in the sitting room. Sierra was already in bed for the evening. The next morning when she woke up and came down the stairs, a majestic seven-foot evergreen tree greeted her. She screamed with delight. Unopened boxes of ornaments lay under the tree as if they were the Christmas gifts. Of course, Sierra wanted to decorate the tree immediately, but I convinced her that she needed to get dressed and eat breakfast first. I had never seen her put on her clothes so quickly or inhale a bowl of cereal with lightning speed.

Hand in hand, we headed to the sitting room. I took the boxes out from under the tree and opened them to reveal our collection of beautiful Christmas ornaments. I reached into the nearest box, retrieved an ornament, and hung it on the tree.

"I can do it, Mama," Sierra chirped, suggesting she wanted to decorate the tree "all by her big self" as we referred to her independent streak.

I retreated back into the kitchen to bake Christmas cookies for the neighbors. Periodically, I

119

would peer through the doorway, which connected the kitchen, and sitting room. Sierra's process was the same for each ornament. She would crouch beside a box and carefully select a bauble, gently holding it in her hands, and carefully turning it in order to enjoy its beauty from all sides. She would stand up, walk gingerly to the tree, and place the ornament in the perfect spot. Then the process would start all over again. This continued for over an hour, which was a long time for a preschooler to maintain her attention on one activity.

I didn't hear a peep out of her. The only sound was the Christmas music I had playing on the stereo and the occasional buzzing sound of the oven timer beckoning me to remove the cookies. I think the holiday tunes and the aroma from the cookies had put me into a trance because I had forgotten to continue to check on Sierra. Suddenly, she was standing beside me looking up into my eyes.

"Come on, Mama. Look!" She took my hand and led me into the sitting room. When I gazed upon the tree, I didn't know whether to laugh or cry. The ornaments usually were placed on the tree from top to bottom and on every side. Today all the ornaments covered just the front of the tree and only as far up as Sierra could reach. The decorations touched each other, each vying for precious tree real estate. The lower branches drooped with the weight of all the treasured trinkets. In contrast, the top branches were bare and perky.

The tree looked so comical, which made me want to laugh. But I knew how much time and effort Sierra had put into decorating it, and that touched my heart and made me want to cry.

"You did this all by yourself?" I questioned my little elf.

"Yep!" she answered as she put her hands on her hips and puffed up her chest with pride.

"It is sooooo beautiful!!" I added.

"I know," Sierra countered nonchalantly.

"Wait until Dad sees this!" I told her.

"He's going to love it!" Sierra said confidently.

I gave her a big hug. She bounded up the stairs. I assumed she wanted to play with the toys in her room. I continued to stand in front of the tree and admire individual ornaments. Suddenly, from out of nowhere, Sierra appeared at my side.

"Here, Mama," she exclaimed as she held out a handmade ornament I had never seen before. It was made of a metal frozen orange juice lid covered in red felt and adorned with silver sequins. Sierra's preschool picture was proudly glued in the center.

"Did you make this at school this week?" I questioned her.

"Yep!" She responded, once again placing her hands on her hips and puffing out her chest with pride.

"You can do it, Mama," she encouraged me as she continued to hold the ornament in front of me. I took the treasured work of art from her tiny hands and hung it on the branch in front of me. It dangled so far above the other ornaments Sierra had placed on the tree. The photo in the center of the ornament looked like a princess overlooking her kingdom of baubles and trinkets. It was perfect. Sierra clapped her hands in delight. I picked her up, and she encircled my neck with her arms for a big hug. I kissed her soft, rosy cheek, and she kissed me back. The buzzing of the oven timer interrupted our touching Christmas moment. I put Sierra down, and we walked hand in hand to the kitchen to enjoy a few of the cookies fresh from the oven.

Reflections
• I could have easily stopped Sierra from decorating the tree by herself for fear that she would break the ornaments. But as a parent I feel it is important to say "yes" more than you say "no." Children build their self-confidence and sense of pride by completing tasks independently.
•Just as Sierra's height determined how high she could place the ornaments on the tree, our development as human beings determine the goals we are able to reach. As she grew, each year Sierra could reach a little higher. As we grow as people, we are able to obtain higher goals in our lives.

You're the One

"If you love something, set it free;
if it come back to you, it's yours.
If it doesn't, it never was yours.

-Richard Bach

My three-year-old daughter, Sierra, was always five steps ahead of me, and today was no exception. The soles of her black patent leather shoes clicked in a familiar pattern on the white tile floor. She was wearing a red print dress with a white collar and cuffs. White, stretchy tights completed her outfit. She clutched a plastic, blue, Fischer Price doctor's bag in her left hand, and wore a yellow plastic stethoscope around her neck. Never in my wildest dreams did I ever imagine she would be wearing the stethoscope or carrying the doctor's bag in an actual hospital. But here we were walking down a hallway at Saint Mary's Hospital in Rochester, Minnesota, heading towards my mother's private room.

It was Christmas morning, but not the Christmas we had planned. For years my husband, Greg, and I had tried to convince my family members who lived in Iowa to come to Colorado for the holidays. We enticed them with visions of breathtaking mountain scenery, a white Christmas with mild weather, a variety of outdoor activities, which included hiking, cross country skiing, snowshoeing, and snowmobiling. The ultimate dangling carrot was spending Christmas in a mountain cabin, curled up by a roaring fireplace with family members making and sharing new memories. It doesn't get any more "Norman Rockwell" than that.

When the family members agreed to the ultimate mountain Christmas experience, we were shocked. Greg didn't waste any time booking several cabins at a resort in Estes Park, for fear if he hesitated, the relatives would change their minds. Everything was set. The cabins were reserved. The menus were planned, and the activities were scheduled. All that was left to do was to wait for the relatives to arrive. Unfortunately, that day never came.

Just days before Christmas, my sister Mary called. Mother had suffered a heart attack followed by several strokes. In order to save her life, Mom had been taken by ambulance from our small hometown in Iowa to Saint Mary's hospital in Rochester, Minnesota.

How could this happen? Mother was such a strong-willed, feisty person. She seemed invincible. She was the one who visited sick people in our small hometown, bringing them meals, and brightening their spirits. She always had some kind of ailment, but she was never really sick herself. At least not sick enough to warrant a hospital stay.

Mary went on to explain what had led to the hospitalization. Mom and Dad had driven to a nearby town to do the grocery shopping for the week. About halfway through the store, Mother started to feel ill. Thinking it was just the flu, they finished the shopping excursion, and drove home.

Mother planted herself on the sofa in the TV room to recover while Dad unpacked the groceries in the kitchen. As the day progressed, Mother's condition worsened until Dad finally called a family friend who had a medical background to come over and take a look at his wife. The friend suspected Mom was having a heart attack and quickly called 911. In minutes, the ambulance with its volunteer firemen and EMTs, all who were either relatives or family friends, arrived to whisk Mom to a small hospital about thirty minutes away. The emergency room doctors quickly decided their hospital was not equipped to save Mother's life, so she was loaded back into the ambulance and rushed to Saint Mary's Medical Center, which is one of the top hospitals in the United States. Currently, Mom was alive but in a coma-like state.

After hanging up the phone and explaining the situation to Greg, we went into action. Greg called the resort in Estes Park to cancel the cabin reservations. The owner was very understanding and offered us his sincere sympathy regarding the situation. I began packing everything we would need for the trip back to Iowa, including all of our Christmas gifts. We left the next morning, driving straight through to Rochester without stopping in Iowa.

We arrived on the afternoon of December 24th. I had been in contact with my sister Mary as we traveled across Nebraska. She had been staying with Dad at a hotel across from the hospital. I could tell by her weary voice that she was exhausted from the stress. I encouraged her to go home in order spend Christmas with her family. She was hesitant but finally agreed. Greg, Sierra, and I would take over her hotel room and stay with Dad. When we arrived, we found my father waiting for us in the hotel lobby. We checked in, unpacked, and headed across the street to the hospital. Dad led us through the maze of hallways to Mother's private room.

I stopped momentarily at the doorway to gather my strength and prepare myself for what I would see. I was glad I did. Mother lay lifeless in the bed. She was attached to several machines, which monitored her heart rate, and other vital signs. I slowly walked to her bedside and bent over to kiss her right cheek. As always, she smelled of Ivory soap, and her skin was amazingly soft and supple for a woman her age. She didn't react to my kiss, so I gently laid my head on her shoulder. As I watched her chest rise and fall with each labored breath, I began to cry. The tears rolled down my face unto her hospital gown, but I didn't care. I had earned the right to weep and even sob for that matter. Not only had I traveled hundreds of miles to be in this hospital room at this very moment, but Mother and I had traveled the highs and lows of life's highways together. Our wills had clashed in the ever-changing mother and daughter relationship we shared. She had always wanted me to stay close, act conservatively, and play it safe. I, on the other hand, longed for adventure. I wanted to see the world, meet interesting people, and do wacky, unexplained things. I lived in large cities by myself, held intriguing jobs, and enjoyed my unique friends. I enjoyed life to the fullest, not in the sense that I partied, drank, did drugs, or broke the law. On the contrary, I was a very law abiding citizen. I just loved adventure and challenges, which made my mother worry. In fact, she often reminded me that I was the cause of the majority of her gray hairs.

I remembered a deep, life changing conversation Mom and I once had. I was a college graduate and had been living on my own for several years when I decided it was time for a "come to Jesus meeting" between Mom and me. I traveled home from Minneapolis to spend a weekend with my parents. Saturday morning after breakfast, I asked Mom to sit at the kitchen table to talk.

"I think it's time for our relationship to change," I began the conversation. "We will always be mother and daughter, but I would like to go beyond that. I would like to be friends."

"I'm not sure what that means," Mom countered.

"I feel like you are always trying to change me and make decisions for me. I know in the past, you needed to keep me safe, to guide me, and influence me because that is part of your job as a mother. But I am a grown up now. I need to make my own decisions and deal with the consequences," I explained.

"I have realized a long time ago that I can't change you. You're too stubborn," Mom replied.

"Hmmm, I wonder where I get that from?" I joked.

"It must be from your dad," she chuckled.

"I know we will always be mother and daughter, but I want to go beyond that. I want to be friends, friends who accept each other without judgment, friends who share common interests, passions, and memories. I think friendship could offer us a relationship with fewer expectations, less stress, and definitely less 'head butting.'" Head butting is what Mother and I called our disagreements.

There was an uncomfortable silence, as Mom looked me in the eyes. I could tell she was mulling over what I had said and was choosing her words carefully. I knew this was difficult for her. She was giving up some of her power. This seemed to happen naturally with her other children on their wedding days, but I wasn't married. At this time in my life, I didn't know if I would ever be married. I did know that I was an adult, and it was time for Mother to let go or at least, rethink how we interacted with each other.

"I can do that," Mother finally answered. "I'm not sure how to be your friend or what it will look like, but I'll try."

"I don't know what it is going to be like, either. But that is all I want you to do, is to try," I reassured her. "Let's just take one day at a time. Agreed?"

"Okay," she promised.

Our relationship did change from that day on. It reminded me of the photographs Mother kept in the black-paged picture albums. In her early life, there were only black and white photos then about the time she was married, people started to add color to photos with a watercolor wash. We were definitely adding color to our otherwise black and white relationship, and the best part was that we were choosing the pigments together.

In a few short months, I invited Mom to accompany me on a trip to Sioux Falls, South Dakota where I was interviewing for a job. Instead of discouraging me from moving again and starting over, she encouraged me to better myself and further my career. After the interview, we explored the city together, looking at neighborhoods where I might live. I had a good feeling about the interview so we spent the afternoon shopping for professional clothes I would need for my new teaching venture. Throughout the day, she shared her opinions, as a friend would, but let me make the decisions.

I did land the job in Sioux Falls, but I only stayed there a year. I was still restless. I had always wanted to live in Colorado, and I had made up my mind that the only way to obtain a job in that state was to live there. Mom helped me find a storage unit for my belongings, then I packed my car with a few items and drove to Colorado to work at a summer camp for handicapped kids. I didn't have employment after the summer, and I knew this worried her. She didn't voice her concern, although I could feel it. She controlled her concern and mustered up encouraging words for me instead.

"You'll find something. I believe in you. I know you can do it," she told me. These were words I had never heard from her before. Usually her comments were full of fear, worry, and caution. "Think about what you are doing. This isn't a good idea. Are you sure about this?" These were the words I usually heard.

I, on the other hand, had the attitude that the greater the risk, the greater the reward. Perhaps,

Mother was beginning to understand my way of thinking. Perhaps, she was beginning to understand me. I thought about the agreement we had made to become friends. We had started coloring our relationship with pale watercolors, always staying within the lines, but now we were choosing brilliant, acrylic pigments splashed across the canvas. I know it was hard for Mother to let me go. I know she wanted desperately to reel me back into the safety of our hometown and to her decision-making. But she had made a promise, and she always kept her word. She knew she had to let me go.

My job at the summer camp ended. Fortunately, I had become friends with the aquatic instructor at camp who was a single parent with two teenagers. She offered me the opportunity to sleep on a mattress in her unfinished basement in exchange for taking care of her kids after school while she was at work. It wasn't the best situation, but at least I wasn't homeless. I was a substitute teacher during the day, and worked at a craft store in the evenings. After a year, I was considered a Colorado resident, and I had stashed away enough money to pay for a semester of graduate school. I moved to Greeley to attend the University of Northern Colorado in order to obtain a master's degree in special education.

I knew the past year had been difficult for Mom. She felt I was going backwards, but I felt I needed to take a step back in order to catapult myself forward. By subbing and working retail for a year, I became a resident and didn't have to pay out of state tuition. Special education teachers were in big demand, not only in Colorado, but across the nation. Earning an advanced degree in this area was going to open many doors for me professionally, if only I was willing to put in the time and make the sacrifice.

The year I lived in my friend's basement, Mother would continually send me care packages. First, there were flannel sheets for my mattress because she knew I was sleeping on a cold cement floor of an unfinished basement. Then it was a pair of wool gloves with a matching scarf to keep me warm when I had recess duty. Many packages contained canned fruit, candy, nuts, granola bars, and home-made cookies. I chuckled thinking perhaps Mother thought we didn't have those foods in Colorado, but I knew it was her way of easing her worry. It was her way of sending me packages of love. I was thankful for the gifts, and I was thankful for the notes of encouragement she included in every box.

During my next visit back home, I expressed my gratitude to her, not only with words, but with a hug and a kiss on the cheek as well. This was a big step in our relationship. Mother was not a person who shared her emotions. We didn't hug very much in our family, and we certainly didn't say the words "I love you." This was just another example of how different the two of us were. I wore my heart on my sleeve, but when I returned home for a visit, I always toned it down a notch for Mom. I felt our relationship was ready to progress a step further, so on the day I left to return back to Colorado, I explained to Mom that every time I left I would like to hug her goodbye and tell her I loved her.

"I would like that," she replied.

It felt very freeing to hear her say those words. I felt like I could finally be myself. It was as if I were the proverbial butterfly emerging from the cocoon.

I floated back to Colorado on cloud nine. In a year, I completed my master's degree, and obtained a job in special education, which paid enough for me to rent a very nice apartment by myself. I no longer lived on the edge of homelessness, sleeping on a mattress on the floor in a friend's basement. I felt I had arrived. I had reached my goal. I had accomplished my dream. I no longer felt restless. Much to my Mother's relief, she felt the same. She knew my wandering days were over, and she was glad about it. In retrospect, I know I would have never made it through those tough years without her care packages, words of encouragement, and constant unconditional love. She was my partner in crime, and my best friend. I loved her even more for being willing to let me go even though it meant worry and stress for her.

All of these memories came flooding back into my mind as if laying my head on her shoulder allowed us to share these thoughts through osmosis. By now the pattern of our breathing had become one. Mother still hadn't moved or spoken; yet somehow I felt we had shared a moment, which didn't require words. She knew I was there, and she knew I loved her. At that moment in time, that was all that was necessary.

I lifted my head from her shoulder, dried my eyes, kissed her cheek, and whispered, " I love you,

Mom." I turned and walked out of the room. Perhaps our journey was meant to end there in a cold, sterile hospital room, but I doubted it. We had come too far to end this way. We had gone from a parent/child relationship to friendship to soulmates. No, this wasn't the end. I didn't know what the future would hold, but I knew in my heart there was something more. There was that restless, uneasy feeling of yearning I had experienced so many times in my life. It entered my body and returned to my very soul. There was something more to this situation that only God and Mother knew. I knew they would share it with me when the time was right. My job was to be patient.

It was Christmas Eve. Dad insisted on buying us a special holiday meal at The Canadian Honker, which was a cozy, dine in restaurant across the street. I knew in the rush of events and decisions to be made in the last few days, that our Christmas gifts from Mom and Dad were back in Iowa, so Dad wanted this lovely meal to be our gift.

As we entered the dining establishment, I noticed every table and booth was occupied. I felt an ache in my heart, knowing most people were eating here because they were in the same situation we were. They had a loved one in the hospital across the street.

Soon warm plates arrived filled with the Christmas Eve special. There were slices of turkey and a mound of creamy, white mashed potatoes accompanied by fluffy, seasoned dressing. Everything was covered with steaming, caramel-colored, turkey gravy. Sierra was overjoyed to be able to munch on her favorite meal of chicken nuggets and French fries while sitting beside her beloved grandfather.

The meal was delicious, yet I couldn't help longing for a bowl of steaming oyster stew. I hated the stuff, with its blobs of gray oyster meat drifting in the milky broth with melted butter creating strange designs on the surface of the soup. Mother had made this delicacy every Christmas Eve for as long as I could remember. It was our family tradition to sip and slurp this soup together on the night before Christmas. I was missing our tradition. I was missing Mom.

We completed our meals with slices of warm apple pie topped with cold, creamy ice cream, then we headed next door to the hotel. Once inside our room, we were presented with a new challenge. Sierra was upset because she felt Santa would not find her on this very special night. She explained to us that Santa always expected her to either be at our home in Colorado or at a grandparent's home. How was he going to find her here?

Her loving grandfather carefully placed Sierra on one of the beds, then gingerly sat beside her.

"Santa Claus always knows where you are, not just on Christmas Eve, but every day," he explained to her. Of course she believed him. She believed everything he ever told her.

Sierra then voiced her concern regarding the fact there wasn't a fireplace in our hotel room. Where was she going to hang her stocking?

"Don't worry," Grandpa Bob reassured her.

"When I was young, we didn't have a fireplace. We put our stockings on our table, and Santa always filled them."

I knew this was true. My father grew up in a family with fifteen kids. They didn't have a fireplace, and even if they did, I can't imagine fifteen stockings hanging around it. They did put their stocking on the table, and every Christmas morning they were overjoyed to find them filled with an orange and a new pair of socks.

"Let's look around this room and find the perfect place to hang your stocking," Dad told Sierra as he lifted her from the bed, and they began looking for the ultimate spot to hang her stocking.

"How about on the window lock?" he asked.

"It's too cold there," she replied. She was right. The window was iced over.

"The doorknob looks like a good place," he offered.

"No, that's not good," she stated without giving a reason.

"How about the handle on this cupboard under the sink?" he pointed out.

"Okay," she agreed.

The two of them proceeded to hang the fuzzy red and white stocking on the cupboard handle. It was during this process that Sierra discovered there were no shelves in the cupboard below the sink. She quickly crawled inside and declared the area her "secret hideout." The not so secret hideout entertained Sierra for the rest of the evening while the grown ups watched TV and talked about the weather and current events. It certainly wasn't the

Christmas Eve we had planned curled up by a roaring fire in the fireplace of a mountain cabin. But at least we were together, and Mother was still alive.

Sierra woke us early the next morning, eager to show us her bulging Christmas stocking and wrapped presents sitting on the floor near her secret hideout door. Santa had found her just as Grandpa Bob had promised. She was elated!

Sierra dumped the contents of her stocking out on the bed to reveal her favorite sweet treats. There were red and white striped peppermint candy canes, individually wrapped taffy, candy bars, chocolate Santas and Christmas bells covered in red and green foil. Sierra was quick to offer a portion of her sugary treasure to Grandpa Bob with the hope that if she was generous and shared, we would allow her to eat candy for breakfast. Of course, her clever plan worked. Besides it was Christmas morning. But wait. There was another stocking lying on the counter by the sink.

"Who is that for?" Sierra inquired.

"I think it's for Grandpa Bob," I explained as I brought the stocking over to the bed. "I doubt that it has an orange and a pair of socks in it, but I think you will like what is inside," I said as I handed it to my dad.

"Well, what do you know, Sierra? Santa Claus not only found you, but he found me as well," Dad rejoiced.

Dad carefully took one item at a time out of the stocking, unlike his hyper granddaughter who simply dumped everything out on the bed. He

136

revealed a bag of Werther's butterscotch candies, a box of Queen Anne's chocolate covered cherries, hard peppermint candies, and several Hershey's Symphony candy bars.

"Sierra, how do you think Santa knows what our favorite candies are?" Dad questioned as he winked at me.

"I don't know. He just does. It's part of his magic," Sierra explained. "Can I open my presents, now?" she asked with a mouth bulging with candy.

Greg brought the gifts to her, gently setting them on the bed. She eagerly ripped off the wrapping paper and squealed with delight at the unveiling of each item. The gifts included a new red dress with a white collar, white tights to match, soft furry mittens with a matching hat, books to read and enjoy, and a stuffed bear to cuddle and love. Finally, she opened the highly anticipated doctor's kit. Immediately, she checked Grandpa Bob's heart with the stethoscope, took his temperature with the thermometer, and gave him an injection in an effort to counteract the mega doses of sugar he had recently ingested.

Once Grandpa's health issues had been resolved, we completed our morning routines, and were ready for the day. Sierra enthusiastically put on her new red dress and white tights. I helped her buckle her black patent leather shoes. She put her yellow stethoscope around her neck, grabbed her blue doctor's bag, and she was ready to go.

We journeyed back to the Canadian Honker for Dad's favorite breakfast of bacon, eggs, and toast. We took advantage of the fact Sierra was willing to do anything we asked as long as she could sit by Grandpa Bob. So when we asked her to put the stethoscope in the doctor's bag while we ate, she didn't argue.

Greg paid the bill, and we made the short journey across the street to the hospital. Once inside, Sierra kept five steps ahead of me. Her black patent leather shoes clicked in a familiar pattern on the white tile floor. Her yellow plastic stethoscope hung around her neck, as she clutched a blue, plastic, Fisher Price doctor bag in her left hand. We quickly reached Mom's room and stepped inside. Nothing had changed. Mom lay motionless still hooked to several machines. I kissed her soft cheek as a friendly, loving hello. There was no response.

I spent the day sitting in a chair by her bed, holding her hand, stroking her arm, and silently praying God would bring her back to all of us, would bring her back to me. Sierra entertained herself with the new toys we had brought along. When she started to get restless, Greg and Dad would take her on an adventure down the hall, which usually ended at the vending machine area where they bought her sweet treats, as if she hadn't eaten enough sugar already. On the trip to and from the vending machines, Dad and Greg would position themselves on either side of the preschooler, grabbing her hands, and lifting her into the air on the count of three. Her giggles echoed through the halls, spreading joy to everyone who could hear.

I was thankful Sierra was oblivious to what was happening to Mom. She simply thought Grandma was asleep. Perhaps, she was merely asleep, her body desperately trying to mend itself through slumber. My worry was what if she never woke up.

It was late in the afternoon on Christmas Day. Dad and Greg had taken Sierra for one last trip down the hall, and I was alone in the room with Mom. Suddenly, her eyes started to flutter. I catapulted myself out of the chair, and immediately leaned over her face.

"Mom, can you hear me?" I sputtered.

She grabbed my shirt collar with such force that it shocked me. She drew my face close to hers.

"You're the one," she whispered. "You're the one!"

Then her eyes closed, and she returned to her slumber. Greg, Dad, and Sierra were standing in the doorway. They saw the shocked look on my face and asked what had happened.

"Mom opened her eyes and said something," I explained.

"What did she say?" Greg asked.

"I'm not sure," I told him. I knew what she had said, but I wasn't sure what it meant.

We were all exhausted from the day, and I needed time to process what Mom had said to me, so I asked if we could leave. Dad and Greg seemed to sense I needed to be alone with Mom one more time, so they took Sierra down the hall. I bent over Mother and kissed her cheek. I hugged her until our breathing took on the same pattern and our hearts beat as one.

"I love you, Mom," I whispered in her ear.

We had made a pact to hug and say I love you each time I left. Today was no exception. It was a ritual we had created as a way for Mom to let me go yet ironically letting go had drawn us even closer. I was glad we had become friends. I was thankful we had time to work on and change our relationship. I was grateful I had taken the chance and asked Mom for what I needed. Throughout my adult life, I had asked Mom to let me go, to let me soar, to let me fly. Ironically, on this Christmas Day, I was the one being asked to let go. I needed to let Mother go so she could soar, so she could fly from this life to the next. Letting go was Mother's way of loving me, now it was my turn. I kissed her cheek, whispered "I love you," and I let go.

I walked out of the room and didn't look back. In the weeks that followed, Mother improved enough to be transported to the nursing home in our hometown. We returned to Colorado, and I called her every Sunday. She never knew who I was, and she rarely made sense when she talked. Even when we returned home to visit her in the summer, she stared at us as if we were complete strangers. It broke my heart to see her as a mere shell of herself, knowing our ties and relationship were gone. But I was grateful I had already let her go. I had already set her free on Christmas Day in Saint Mary's Hospital.

Mom lived at the nursing home until she journeyed to heaven on Halloween, which ironically was one of her favorite holidays. It was so like her to plan her departure in such a manner.

For years I contemplated the last words she spoke to me.

"You're the one".

What did that mean? Why did she say it? Was she even coherent at the time? I refused to believe those words were just babbling. They had meaning. They had to. But what?

The answer came to me years later. I was sitting in the silence of church before Sunday mass began, praying for Mom when those final words echoed through my memory as they often did.

You're the one means you are special and chosen. That was the message Mom and my other parent, God the Father, was sending to me. I was special. I had been chosen, but chosen for what? Therein lies the beauty in what she had said to me. It was deliberately left open-ended, left for me to find my purpose. Through the process of finding myself, my calling, my talents, my reason for being, I changed, grew, and morphed into the person I was meant to become. It reminded me of mountain climbing in Colorado. Sure the view from a mountaintop is fabulous, but really it is all about the climb. The actual process of hiking a mountain does wonders for your self-concept. It's all about believing in yourself. Not giving up. Keeping the goal in sight. The process truly changes you. It really is all about the climb.

I thought about how Mom and I had vibrantly colored our relationship with love, understanding, and encouragement. With her final words she handed the paintbrush to me to finish the masterpiece of our relationship.

"You're the one. Carry on sweet daughter. Celebrate your uniqueness. Never give up your sense of adventure. I believe in you. Continue what we have started. You have the skills. You can do it because . . . you're the one. "

In seems that so many times in our lives we are afraid to let something go. We're afraid to let go of the structure and comfort of what we already know in exchange for an uncertain future. Simply put, we trade certainty for possibilities. That is a frightening proposition no matter how brave you think you are. I must admit by letting go of life's certainties, the rewards and possibilities have exceeded my wildest expectations.

Reflections

•The friendship with my mother was living proof that relationships can be purposely built by discussing the goals and expectations with the people involved.

•A few encouraging words from someone you love can give you the strength to continue to scale the mountains before you and to realize it's not about reaching the mountaintop. It's all about the climb.

•There is a beautiful bond between a mother and daughter that can never be broken even by death.

•Sometimes letting go can draw people closer together.

Adventure calls and Mom says goodbye

My Superman

"A hero is an ordinary individual who finds the strength to persevere and endure in spite of overwhelming obstacles."

-Christopher Reeves a.k.a. Superman

For most people Superman is a mythical character dreamed up by a group of comic book writers and filmmakers. For me, Superman was real. The truth of the matter was that I had my own personal Superman, my brother Steve.

Steve was ten years older than I was. His brown eyes, dark hair, muscular build, and mischievous grin made him extremely handsome. He was intelligent, witty, and friendly. Steve never met a stranger. People loved him. When I was a young girl, he would often give me advice and words of encouragement, which I treasured as if his words were pieces of gold.

In the movies and comics, even with all of his super human powers, Superman had something that deprived him of his strength. That something was kryptonite. My Superman's kryptonite was cancer, colon cancer. As any super hero would, Steve fought the battle against cancer with all the strength he could muster physically and emotionally. Over the span of several years, he faced many surgeries and chemotherapy treatments with stamina, humor, and grace. I never heard him complain, whine, or grumble. He just took one day at a time and did what he needed to do. As I watched his life unfold, my admiration for him grew. He truly was my Superman.

Halloween and Christmas were my mother's favorite holidays. Ironically my mother passed away on October 31, 1998. Her funeral was in early November, so my family and I traveled back to Iowa to attend the service and say goodbye. Because we had just journeyed to the Midwest in November, we decided to spend Christmas at home in Colorado.

When I couldn't be in Iowa for the holidays, I would call my parents' home on Christmas afternoon because that was where and when everyone gathered to celebrate. My family members would take turns talking to me on the phone, filling me in on their Christmas gifts and activities, as well as the news in our small hometown. I knew this year would be heartbreaking because it was our first Christmas without Mom, but I really had no idea how sad and different it was going to be.

I was somewhat surprised when my sister Mary answered the phone at Dad's house that Christmas afternoon. I could tell by the tone of her voice that something was terribly wrong. When I asked her what was the matter, the floodgates opened, and everything came spilling out.

After the food was eaten, and the gifts were opened, Steve shared with everyone that the doctors could no longer help him battle cancer. There would be no more surgeries, no more chemo treatments, and this would be the last Christmas he would spend with the family. The doctors had told him he had a month or two to live.

Christmas seemed like an unusual time to share such gut-wrenching news, but I could understand Steve's reasoning. Christmas was the one time during the year we were all together. This way he could explain his situation once for everyone to hear. The thought of repeating the sad news to each family member was unbearable.

I asked to speak to Steve, but Mary told me he had already left, as did everyone else. Unable to choke back the tears, my sister and I decided to say goodbye. I sat with the phone still in my hand, wallowing in my own sorrow and disbelief. How could this happen to my Superman? He was so strong, and so invincible. He had been a warrior against cancer for many years, and he deserved to win this battle. He didn't deserve for his life to end this way.

The next two weeks were a blur. I vaguely remember calling Steve and asking if I could come home to visit him. I didn't want to make him feel uncomfortable, but I knew I needed to see him in person to say goodbye.

I was able to take a week off from work in January to fly back for a visit. Dad and Steve were always my "go to guys" when I needed someone to pick me up or drop me off at the airport. This time Steve wasn't there to greet me. It seemed surreal when Dad and one of my sisters met me at the gate. My flight had arrived late in the evening, so we drove to my father's home in Northern Iowa in darkness and silence, too sad and tired to speak.

The next day, I accepted Dad's offer to take me to Steve's home in a small town about eight miles away. Dad drove. I rode shotgun, and my three sisters piled into the backseat. When we arrived, Steve was in the basement relaxing in his recliner because he was too weak to stand. We each took turns bending over to hug him. When it was my turn to give my bother a squeeze, I felt his bones in my grasp. The cancer seemed to have eaten away his muscles. His once tan skin was now pale and wrapped loosely around his bones. His body was different, but his face hadn't changed. His thick, dark hair remained the same, as did his big, brown eyes and boyish grin. Miraculously, throughout his chemotherapy treatments Steve had never lost his hair.

After the "hug fest," Dad and my sisters squeezed themselves onto the couch, and I took up residence in the nearby cushioned chair. Dad started the conversation with complaints about the cold temperatures and the possibility of an impending snowstorm. My sisters chimed in with accounts of winter weather from the past.

I didn't take part in the weather related verbal exchange. I simply stared in disbelief at my relatives sitting on the couch discussing meteorological conditions. I hadn't traveled hundreds of miles to talk about the weather. The situation was what my boss referred to as "having an elephant in the room." In other words, there was clearly an issue, which needed to be addressed, but no one wanted to acknowledge it. The elephant was Steve was dying.

I wanted to talk to Steve about what he was going through and what he was feeling. Instead, we were discussing outdoor temperatures and precipitation. Although our conversation was mundane, the visit seemed to go by quickly, and soon we were hugging Steve goodbye.

The next morning during breakfast, I asked Dad if I could borrow his car for the day.

"Sure, I'm not going anywhere," he replied. "Where are you going?"

"I'm going to visit Steve, but I want to go alone this time," I answered.

"I understand," Dad assured me as he handed me the car keys.

After breakfast, I drove to Steve's home in silence, internally praying I would know what to say to my precious brother. Once I arrived, God seemed to take over the conversation. It all began with one simple question.

"Steve, are you afraid of dying?" I asked.

"No," he responded. That was exactly what I had expected him to say. In my world he was Superman, and of course Superman isn't afraid of anything. Steve continued to explain his answer.

"I was afraid of dying at first," my brother continued. "Then I started experiencing something strange but strange in a good way. It seems to happen when I'm right on the verge of being awake and being asleep."

"I know what you mean. Tell me more," I encouraged him.

"It's hard to explain, but I'll try. It's like I no longer have a body, and I am floating in space. It's

147

dark but not cold. There are rays of light, which are like stars but not really. Each light is a person who talks to me. Each person wants me to come with them, telling me it is so peaceful where they exist. But each time this happens, I tell them I am not ready yet."

"Is Chad one of those people?" I asked him. Chad was Steve's son who had died in a motorcycle accident at the age of seventeen.

"No, I was hoping it would be Chad, but it wasn't."

"I'm sorry," I whispered trying to comfort my brother. "When Mom was sick I read a book about dying that was written by a hospice nurse. She said many people would see a family member who was deceased, and that person would be their guide from this world to the next."

"I've heard of that, too," Steve responded. "That's why I was hoping it would be Chad. I'd give anything to see him one more time."

"It could still happen," I assured him. "How many times have you experienced this situation?"

"Twice. Both times it was so peaceful and relaxing. I have to admit I was tempted to go with them, but I knew I couldn't. I can't explain why. I just knew I wasn't ready."

"It will happen when the time is right."

"I know that's true, and that's why I'm not afraid anymore," he assured me.

At that moment, I felt as if a weight had been taken off my shoulders. I didn't want Steve to be afraid. If he had to die, I wanted him to die in peace. To tell the truth I was afraid of dying until I heard Steve speak about his experience. Now, not only his fear was gone, but so was mine.

I felt much more satisfied with this conversation than I did with the one from the previous day. I had been watching my brother carefully and could tell he was getting tired. I hugged him goodbye and asked if I could visit him the next afternoon. He agreed, and I left.

The next day, we talked about God. Steve shared his belief that God is everywhere not just in churches. He also explained he believed you could talk to God anywhere and at anytime. You didn't always need to say a prayer, just talk to Him like He was a regular person. I must admit, I liked his ideas which were simple yet brilliant.

At one point in the conversation, he said one of his friends had asked him why he didn't go to church on Sundays. Steve's response was, "I'd rather be on a lake fishing and thinking about God than be in a church thinking about fishing." It made a lot of sense to me. It made me remember just how very smart my Superman was.

The week continued in a similar fashion. I would arrive in the afternoon, and we would discuss whatever topic Steve wanted to explore. One day we reminisced about our favorite memories of growing up on our farm. We shared funny stories about Mom, Dad, and our siblings. I laughed so hard that my stomach hurt and tears rolled down my cheeks.

On my final visit, I asked Steve if he had any regrets. Was there anything he wanted to do that he had not been able to experience? He told me he wished he hadn't spent so much money on his fishing equipment, on things like fish finders, and boats. Instead he wished he would have taken that money and gone on trips with his wife, Jane. When I asked him where he would want to go, he responded, "Anywhere." I assured him if that was his only regret, then he had lived an awesome life. He agreed. He felt he had lived a wonderful life. He had a wife who was his soulmate and two sons who were his pride and joy. What more could a man ask for?

As our conversation neared its end, Steve asked me to make a promise to him. Of course, my response was yes. How could I refuse my beloved brother? Even though I was still in my thirties, he wanted me to promise to have a colonoscopy, which was a test most people didn't have until age fifty. As I looked at my forty-eight year old brother for the last time, I knew he was right. He was always right. I needed to be tested and so did the rest of our siblings. This request was so like Steve. I had returned home to visit and comfort him, but in the end, he turned the tables and made the situation to be about me. He was always the protective big brother looking out for his little sister.

It was hard to leave that day knowing it would be the last time I would see or touch my big brother. Steve and I both rose from our chairs in order to hug each other. Our embrace lasted several minutes, neither of us wanting to let go. Finally, I whispered in his ear, "I love you, Steve. You are my Superman." He squeezed me as tightly as he could. As I let him go, I saw big tears in his eyes, and I knew he couldn't speak. Maybe we had spoken enough over the past week. Maybe this was a situation in which no words were necessary. I squeezed his hand, said goodbye, and left. I knew I couldn't turn around for fear that I would run back to hug him again. I knew it was time to let go.

I cried all the way back to Dad's house. The tears rolled down my face in salty streams. At times, it was difficult to see the highway. My eyes were blurry, and memories of Steve flashed through my imagination like images on a movie screen. I tried to imagine life without Steve, but it wasn't in my realm of thinking. Steve had always been in my life. When I reached my parents' home, I parked the car in the garage, and scurried to my bedroom. I didn't want Dad to see my tear-stained face. He never did well with crying.

I flew back to Colorado the following morning. Steve joined the people of the twinkling lights in their peaceful existence on February 23, 1999. He must have known the time was right. I kept my promise and convinced my doctor to allow me to have a colonoscopy at the age of thirty-eight. I was glad I did. A polyp was found and removed from my colon. If it had not been removed, it could have easily turned into a malignant tumor. I was scheduled to have a colonoscopy every year for the next five years. While I was being tested, I decided to also have a mammogram even though I wasn't forty years old yet. Once again, I was grateful to my brother for the promise he asked me to make. A suspicious spot was found on my breast. My doctors continued to monitor it for several years.

Eventually, the spot was biopsied and found to be malignant, but thanks to early detection, thanks to the promise I made to Steve, I became a cancer survivor.

Just as the mythical Superman saved the lives of many people, my Superman saved lives as well. There is one life in particular that I am so very grateful that he saved . . . mine.

Reflections
•I learned not to be afraid of dying.
•I learned the importance of talking about what is important.
•I learned to live your life with no regrets.

Steve, My Superman

Mother Would Have
Wanted It That Way

*"Grief never ends, but it changes. It's a passage,
not a place to stay. Grief is not a sign of weakness,
not a lack of faith. It is the price of love."*
                                    -Author Unknown

Mother was a strong-willed person with a delightful sense of humor. Throughout her life, she always got what she wanted, not in a demanding way, but with her stern yet patient demeanor.

Mother had suffered a heart attack followed by several strokes right before Christmas in 1997. She spent several months in a nursing home until she passed away on Halloween the following year. Christmas had been a sad and lonely holiday for my family for the last two years. This year seemed to continue the pattern in that my older brother, Steve, had lost his battle with cancer, and had passed away in February 1999. Needless to say, my family was hesitant about "celebrating" Christmas. Our sense of loss was too deep and too raw.

I lived in Colorado with my husband, Greg, and our preschool-aged daughter, Sierra. Due to the distance and time constraints of our jobs, we were unable to journey back to Iowa for Thanksgiving, which made me eager and anxious to be with my family at Christmas. In an effort to convince my siblings to gather together one more time, I volunteered to host Christmas dinner at Dad's home. Perhaps it was my persuasive nature, also known as whining, or my cooking skills that

153

convinced the relatives to agree to share Christmas dinner together.

Due to our work schedules, Greg and I were unable to leave Colorado as early as we had wished. We estimated that we would arrive in Iowa two days before Christmas, and that was not allowing for winter weather conditions, which could add hours or even days to the drive across Nebraska. Arriving two days before the holiday didn't seem like a problem until we thought about purchasing and preparing the food for the Christmas feast. My hometown only had a small country store where the local residents could buy a gallon of milk or a loaf of bread. We would need to drive several miles to a larger city to acquire enough food for a feast that would feed over thirty people.

With all of these pieces of information in mind, Greg and I decided to purchase the food in Colorado and transport it to Iowa. We packed our vehicle as if it were a three-dimensional puzzle, using every bit of available space. The cargo area was filled with suitcases, boxes of food, and a giant, green Coleman cooler, which contained the largest turkey we could purchase. Sierra's car seat was nestled in the backseat surrounded by brightly wrapped Christmas gifts. Sierra squealed with delight as we buckled her into the car seat. She was excited to be surrounded by the beautifully wrapped presents. We always thought of Sierra as a gift, but this year her very presence at my parent's Iowa home would be a gift to her precious grandfather who was still recovering from the loss of his wife and son.

As the prairie wind howled and the gritty snow blew across the highway in waves, I tried to imagine Christmas without Mom and Steve. Each year Mother would position herself on the small sofa by the front window, an hour before our estimated arrival time. Like a sentinel, she would patiently wait for our car to pull into the driveway, then she would rush to the garage door to greet us with hugs that warmed our hearts and kisses that left bright red lipstick smudges on our cheeks. This time, there would be no welcome home greeting from Mom, and there never would be again. A wave of grief and sorrow rushed over my soul. As I stared out of the car window at the bleak Nebraska countryside, I questioned whether my life without Mom was going to be as stark and empty as the winter landscape that surrounded me. I was determined not to let that happen. Mother wouldn't have wanted it that way. That was why this journey was so important. I knew everyone was at different stages in the grieving process. Our hearts were broken, and the best way for all of us to begin to heal those wounds would be for us to be together at Christmas.

The sun had already set when we pulled into the driveway of my Dad's home. Mom's silhouette was missing from the front window, but every light in the house was on, and the warm glow welcomed us and beckoned us to enter.

Our entrance awakened Dad from his slumber in his recliner. He jumped to his feet to hug us, squeezing his precious granddaughter first. After hugs all around, Sierra snuggled up on Grandpa

Bob's lap to watch television while Greg and I unpacked the car.

A quick glance at the contents of the refrigerator made me glad we had brought along more than just the food for the Christmas meal. It was clear that Dad had been living on ham sandwiches and eggs. When the car was finally unpacked, we woke Sierra and Dad from the recliner in the living room, and we all headed off to bed.

We awoke the next morning to the sound of bacon crackling in a frying pan on the stove. In our family, bacon is a form of ambrosia. Frying a pan of the delectable strips of pork was an act of love and kindness. Still in our pajamas, we followed the smoky aroma to the kitchen. There we found Dad dressed in a shirt and jeans. Unlike us, he would never roam the house in his pajamas. He quickly flipped the sizzling bacon onto a plate covered with a paper towel and retrieved a bowl of steaming scrambled eggs from the microwave. His chest puffed with pride at his culinary skills as he proclaimed, "Let's eat!"

Sierra plopped into the chair beside Grandpa Bob. She always felt that being in close proximity to her cherished grandfather was a prize she had earned for good behavior. Throughout breakfast, she watched his every move, gazing at him as if she couldn't believe he was real. Frequently, he would glance at her and include her in the conversation. Her joy from the attention was transformed into a glorious smile that would melt anyone's heart, but especially Grandpa Bob's.

156

We savored every morsel of the protein packed breakfast, as we exclaimed adjectives regarding the delicious taste of the meal. This made the cook beam with satisfaction. As soon as the kitchen was cleaned, and everyone was dressed, we began our tasks for the day. Sierra and Grandpa Bob settled into the living room, ready to educate each other on the entertainment value of their favorite television programs. Grandpa shared his list of "must see" shows, which included All Star Wrestling, Lawrence Welk reruns, and the local news. Sierra shared her love of Sesame Street, Barney, and Looney Tune cartoons. Needless to say, they had plans of spending the day laughing in front of the tube, eating junk food and Christmas cookies.

Greg and I had assigned ourselves the overwhelming task of transforming the basement into a Christmas wonderland. This was a challenging undertaking considering the environment we had to start with. Fortunately, it was a finished basement, but I use the term "finished" loosely. Greg and I headed down to the lower level of my parent's ranch style home. At the bottom of the stairs, Greg flipped on the light switch.

"Oh my God," I whispered, not as an expletive but as an actual prayer. It was going to take an act of God and lots of elbow grease to transform the cold, damp, dark cave into a room filled with Christmas spirit.

As high school students, my brother and I loved the low ceiling in the basement because we could touch it, which made us feel tall and grown up.

Now that I was a grown up, the low ceiling made me feel claustrophobic, and it added to the cave-like feel of the room. Only the south side had small windows near the ceiling. This was a great design in terms of safety. There were many instances when my family had taken refuge in the basement during dramatic windstorms, tornado watches, and warnings. We felt safe in our little hole in the ground. In those circumstances, the fewer the windows, the better. But the design in terms of decorating was challenging. The miniscule windows allowed little natural light to enter the indoor space, and Mother had chosen brown, burlap bags as window coverings, which only darkened the atmosphere even more. Another contributing factor to the gloominess of the room was the fact that the walls were covered with wood paneling rather than painted drywall. The carpet on the other hand was anything but gloomy. It was low cut and included every color of the rainbow.

The furnishings didn't do much to enhance the ambience either. Upon entering, it was unclear whether you were in the room of someone's home or at a used furniture store. A multitude of mismatched, worn chairs from the last fifty years lined the perimeter of the space along with two couches, which were covered with ugly, orange upholstery material from the sixties. The center of the room was consumed by a mysterious, giant pool table. It was mysterious because no one in our family ever played pool. Being the resourceful person she was, my mom found many uses for the table. She slapped on huge piece of plywood on the top of it, and used it as a quilting frame. Later in life, she and Dad bought a toy train that chugged around the edge of the plywood, and through the small village they had created in the middle.

The best use of the table was that it was where all the kids ate Christmas dinner each year. The grown ups would eat upstairs, but due to a lack of space, the grandkids were always banished to the basement. The grown ups liked this situation because the kids were out of sight and out of mind, but the kids thought the basement was cold, damp, dark, and scary. Not exactly words you would use to describe Christmas at your grandparents' home. This year I was determined to change that tradition. This year, we were all going to be together. We were all going to dine in the basement, all thirty-five of us. Perhaps it was an insurmountable task, but Christmas miracles have been known to happen or at least that was what I was counting on.

There are projects you work on, and you know exactly what the end product is going to look like before you even begin. Those projects are often easy to start because you have a goal or target to work toward. Transforming the basement was not one of those projects. I didn't have a visual picture of what I wanted the room to look like in the end. Without that goal, starting was difficult. Then I remembered many situations in life are like that. You don't know the outcome of all relationships, endeavors, or projects. The end product evolves as you work through the process. In some situations the target is never reached, the process never ends, but neither does the learning. Maybe that was the case for this situation. I needed to overcome my fear of failure. I needed to stop thinking about the sorrow everyone was feeling, and concentrate on how much our mother loved Christmas. Obviously, she wasn't going to be with us physically, but there was no reason she couldn't be with us emotionally or spiritually. I used those thoughts as my inspiration. How could this room evoke not only the spirit of Christmas, but my mother's spirit as well? What were the things that Mother loved about Christmas? Christmas music. She loved the classics sang by crooners like Bing Crosby, Frank Sinatra, and Rosemary Clooney. I spied a clock radio on the built-in bookshelves by the stairs. I quickly found a station that played uninterrupted Christmas tunes. Soon the creative juices started flowing, and the magic began.

As empty nesters, my parents only used the basement for a storage area. To save money on the heating bill, Dad had closed all of the heat vents. Greg circulated around the room opening the vents. Soon we were able to trade in the adjectives cold and damp for warm, dry, and toasty. If only the other problems we faced could be so easily solved.

Keeping in mind what my mother liked, moved us to the next stage of the process. Mother kept her house immaculately clean and organized. While I scrubbed everything with Pine Sol, Greg fixed the broken chairs and furniture, cleared the top of the pool table, and set up several folding tables.

As I was dusting the built-in bookshelves, I realized the shelves had become an area where Mom had put items she didn't know what to do with. There were many broken toys, scratched and dented knickknacks, partially burned candles, jars without lids, and faded plastic flowers. These were probably things that had emotional meaning for her, and she was unable to throw them away. But were these items she treasured and cherished? I doubted it. I wasn't going to throw away her belongings. That wasn't my place, so I carefully packed them up and carried the box into the storage area in the furnace room.

I wanted the bookshelf to be the showcase of what my mother treasured the most, her family,   so I scoured the house in search of family snapshots, and finally hit the jackpot when I found boxes of framed photos and photo albums in the closet of my old bedroom. I envisioned the bookshelf as a giant picture book that told the story of our family with photographs. Fortunately, the bookshelf was massive. It covered an entire wall from ceiling to floor.

I started at the upper left shelf with Mom and Dad's wedding picture and worked my way across the top shelf with photos of my siblings intermixed with family photos and anniversary pictures throughout the years. The middle shelves were filled with the smiling faces of grandchildren, and trips my parents had taken. The bottom shelf marked the end of the story with photos of great grandchildren. As I peered at the finished display, I realized that my mother had lived a wonderful life, and that made me happy. Even though I loved the story the bookshelf told, I felt that something was missing. I wanted that area of the room to be the focal point, but how could that be accomplished? What else did Mother love about Christmas? Lights! She loved Christmas lights. Each year Mother and Dad covered our house inside and out with thousands of glowing bulbs.

As if on cue, Greg emerged from the furnace storage room dragging two boxes labeled Christmas lights and ornaments. "There are a lot more where these came from," he informed me. As I opened the boxes, Greg continued to haul out more. It was as if we had discovered buried treasure. Instead of precious metals and gems, we had found lights of every shape, size, and color as well as Christmas ornaments and decorations that told our family's history.

I immediately began to work on the bookshelf, outlining it with white lights and intertwining the strings between the photographs. The white lights seemed symbolic of God's love joining us together through the years. Beside each photograph, I placed an ornament from the various stages of our family's timeline. There were elves made of felt, Santa and angel statues, plastic holly leaves and berries, tree ornaments with our school pictures glued in the centers, and plaster handprints of the grandchildren. The bookshelf had not only become the focal point of the room, it was the very heart of the environment. Just like a heart, it was the place where all the memories and emotions were stored. Just as arteries extend out from a heart, I wanted the lights to extend the spirit of our family, the spirit of Christmas, Mom's spirit. Greg and I hung the strings of bright bulbs around the entire room where the walls met the ceiling. An added side effect was that the lights created the illusion that the ceiling was actually taller. In the end, the desired effect was achieved. The dark and gloomy atmosphere was transformed into an environment of light and hope.

To continue the theme of light and hope, we removed the burlap curtains and draped the window frames with evergreen boughs and icicle lights. The evergreen boughs looked spectacular around the windows, so we decided to use the greenery as a unifying theme throughout the space. We wrapped the lamp stands, adorned the top of the coffee tables, but most importantly, we wrapped all the mismatched chairs with the fake, green plant material. As a contrasting touch, we added red velvet ribbons and plastic poinsettia blossoms to the chairs. Mother loved those two Christmas decorations, and she had purchased them in bulk through the years. We quickly emptied the remaining boxes, sprinkling ornaments and decorations throughout the room.

Our final task was to set the tables. We started with white, red, and green tablecloths, which was the easy part. The challenge was that we did not have place settings for thirty-five people. Greg suggested paper plates and cups, but I wanted the real stuff. The room had started out looking like a garage sale, but in the end I wanted it to have a touch of class. I gathered every plate, glass, and piece of silverware including the items in a wicker picnic basket that Mother kept in the storage room. As I looked at the collection of tableware, I decided mismatched was the theme, and I started to randomly set out the plates, glasses, and silverware. At first, it was odd to see white china next to brightly colored plastic picnic plates, but soon it began to look fun, funky maybe even a little shabby chic.

Throughout the day, we had stopped to make lunch and dinner. We managed to share these meals with Dad and Sierra, and we also managed to take time for needed and well-deserved breaks. By 10 p.m., Greg and I were exhausted. I convinced Greg to go upstairs and go to sleep while I put the finishing touches on the room.

An idea had been brewing in my head the entire day. I wanted to create a snowstorm in the basement. I began cutting hundreds of paper snowflakes in various sizes, then I connected them with fishing line. Three or four flakes completed each string, which was attached to the ceiling with a thumbtack. The clear filament of the fishing line created the illusion that the snowflakes were actually floating in mid-air, but that wasn't the magical part. The magic was the bottom snowflakes on selected strings contained the names of family members. I wanted the paper snowstorm to represent our family. Just as individual snowflakes create a storm, each individual person created our family. Just as no two snowflakes are alike, each person has his/her own personality. Yet each of us had something in common, a little bit of my mother, not only in our DNA, but also in our personalities. We all had her work ethic, her "can do" attitude, her stubborn streak, her creativity, her sense of generosity and empathy, her belief in God, and her delightful sense of humor. We all had a little bit of her "flakiness." Even though we were distinctively different, inherently we were all the same.

As I sat in the middle of the floor on the rainbow carpet surrounded by paper scraps, I surveyed the room. I longed to show my mother what Greg and I had created that day. It was a memorial to her and her love of Christmas. I longed to throw my arms around her neck, to kiss her cheek, to hug her so tightly that our hearts seemed to beat in the same rhythm. I longed to thank her for all she had done for me, for giving me life, for teaching me values, for being my biggest cheerleader, for letting me soar even when she feared for my safety, and for loving me at my most unlovable moments. Those physical longings would never be satisfied. I would never touch her again. I would never hear her wonderful laugh, or carry on a conversation with her. A tear moistened my cheek and soon many more followed. I let them flow. Now was the time to cry, not when the family members arrived on Christmas Day. That would be the time for celebration. It would be a celebration of Mother, her life, her wacky personality, and her love of Christmas. The trance-like state I was in suddenly broke when Greg called my name from the top of the stairs.

"I'll be right up," I answered as I dried my tears on my shirtsleeves. When I reached the upper level I looked at the clock and realized it was 2 a.m. The snowflake project I had thought would take a couple of hours had taken several. I was so caught up in the moment that I had lost track of time. I didn't mind giving up a few hours of sleep. The time spent had helped me heal, and that was exactly what I needed to survive, to go on, to live. Mother would have wanted it that way.

The next day was Christmas Eve. I was so busy preparing the food that I completely forgot about the basement. There were potatoes to peel, stuffing to season, cookies to bake, salads to make, and desserts to create. These were all tasks Mother and I had done together for as long as I could remember. On this day, I completed the tasks solo knowing that she had taught me well. Thanks to her help and guidance, I was ready to fly on my own. That evening we attended midnight mass, returned home to snuggle in our beds, and await Santa's arrival.

Of course, Sierra was up at sunrise eager to discover what Santa had given her. She spent most of the morning playing with her new toys and loving on Grandpa Bob while I put the finishing touches on the food. The guests started to arrive around noon as we had planned to eat the midday meal at 1 o'clock. My sister Mary and her family were the first to arrive. She surveyed the upstairs living area with a questioning glance. I knew exactly what she was thinking. I always did. There were no tables set up, no sign of Christmas except for the Christmas tree in the corner by the TV.

"We're eating in the basement," I explained. She looked at me with a raised eyebrow as if to say, "You have got to be kidding me."

"Let's take the food you've brought and put it down there on the table," I assured her as I lead the way down to the basement. When we reached the bottom of the stairs I switched on the lights.

"Oh my God," my sister exclaimed. This time the phrase was an expletive not a prayer. I led her around the corner to the bookshelf. As we looked at the photos of our family's timeline, I slipped my arm around her waist, and she rested her arm across my shoulders. We squeezed each other tightly. We set her food on the pool table and ventured upstairs to greet the rest of the guests.

The day turned out to be all that I had hoped for and more. A steady stream of relatives arrived from noon until one. Many of them asked where to put the food and gifts they had brought. When I responded, "Just take everything to the basement," I was met with raised eyebrows, gaping mouths, and questioning glances. Once people ventured to the basement, they never returned to the upper level. I took that as a good omen. At least they weren't trying to escape from the once dark, damp, and scary dungeon.

In fact, as I continued to carry the food from the kitchen to the lower level, I noticed relatives were clustered in small groups throughout the room. Many were admiring the decorations that reminded them of Christmas stories from the past. I overheard conversations like; "I remember how Mom always put the felt elves around our family picture each year. It made me laugh because it was like the elves were part of our family." Or "I made this ornament for Mom when I was in fifth grade. I had no idea that she had kept it all these years." Or "Mom always loved plastic poinsettias especially when they were sprinkled with silver glitter." Or "Mom would have loved all of these Christmas lights. Remember how she kept the lights up on the outside of our old farmhouse all year long? She would flash them on and off when we weren't riding the school bus to tell the driver to move on to the next stop." Each shared memory would ignite a chain reaction of laughter. I was happy because Mother would have wanted it that way.

Soon all the guests had arrived, so I invited everyone to the tables. "You see your spouse and kids everyday, so take this opportunity to sit by someone new this year," I challenged them. These were Midwesterners, creatures of habit, and lovers of tradition. First, I had gathered them all in the basement, including the kids, and now I was asking them to sit next to someone new. I was hoping my request wouldn't push them over the edge of what they considered to be sanity, but to my surprise everyone accepted the challenge and actually enjoyed it. There were many multigenerational conversations going on as we enjoyed our delicious imported Christmas delicacies. Older relatives were sharing stories of monstrous, dangerous Christmas snowstorms, and the unsolved mystery of why our Mother made us eat oyster stew every Christmas Eve when she knew we all hated that creamy white soup with a passion. The kids were talking about their favorite holiday candies and desserts Grandma made, and the Christmas gift she always gave them . . .McDonald's gift certificates. What kid doesn't

168

love McDonald's? She always knew what the kids liked because no matter how old she was; she was always a kid at heart.

I must admit that the food was delicious, but that didn't really matter. We could have been eating bricks and rocks, and no one would have even noticed. They were too involved and entranced by each other. Sharing stories, conversations, memories, laughter, and each other's company was the greatest gift they could have given to each other, but we also had physical gifts to exchange after the meal. After stuffing ourselves with the holiday food, everyone helped clean off the tables, carry the leftovers and tableware upstairs. Then we moved our evergreen covered chairs to the perimeter of the room. We all knew the drill. Mother had taught us well.

Because the members of our family had reached over thirty in number, we had been drawing names for Christmas for several years. This year was no exception. A pile of gifts had been created near the bottom of the stairs, and several of the teenaged granddaughters had designated themselves as elves, who placed packages in front of each person. Every year each family member would receive two gifts; one from the person who had drawn their name and one from Mom and Dad (a.k.a. Grandma and Grandpa). For years, we had tried to convince Mom to just participate in the name drawing and not purchase a gift for every family member. We thought it was getting to be too much for her, but little did we realize how much she enjoyed buying gifts for each of us and watching us open them on

Christmas Day. All of this was ironic because in an effort to maintain fairness, she bought all of us the same gift every year. The women received turtleneck sweaters, and flannel shirts were the standard gifts for the men. Of course, the grandkids under the age of eighteen, delighted in receiving McDonald's gift certificates.

As the elves completed their task of delivering the gifts to each person, I was surprised to see that everyone had two gifts in front of them. I only expected one, the one from the name drawing. I grasped one of the gifts in front of me. I knew from years of experience, from the shape and how it squished in my hands that the colorful Christmas wrapping contained a turtleneck sweater. I glanced at the nametag to see my name scrawled in Dad's wiggly, cursive handwriting. From Mom and Dad the tag read. I glanced up and across the room at Dad's face. He gave me a wink and a flash of his famous unforgettable smile.

It was our tradition to open the gifts one person at a time so everyone could see what had been given and to "ew and ah" about the contents of each package. We always started with the youngest person and worked our way to the oldest family member. We would continue in this fashion until all the gifts had been opened. It was hard to skip Mother and Steve's turns as we went around the circle. We could all feel the pain and sense of loss. When it came time for everyone to open the gifts Dad had purchased for each of us, the pain seemed to lessen. Once again, as we did every year, we reveled in our turtlenecks sweaters, flannel shirts, and McDonald's gift certificates. It was as if Mother was there in the room with a big smile of satisfaction spread across her face.

As the teenaged elves deposited crumpled wrapping paper into garbage bags, I strolled across the room towards my father. Once I reached him, I put my arms around his neck, and whispered, "Thanks, Dad."

While the adults enjoyed desserts and visited with each other, the kids colored Christmas images and munched on cookies. I was pleasantly surprised that some of the college-aged grandkids joined in the coloring contest. Of course, Grandpa Bob was the judge of the contest, and he wisely proclaimed that everyone was a winner. The prizes consisted of Christmas candy, cookies, and a live concert performed by Grandpa Bob and his harmonica. My dad knew approximately five songs on the harmonica, none of which were Christmas songs, but that didn't matter. We loved the musician and the music. The grandkids danced around the room as he played, and we all wildly applauded at the end of each song. Dancing and singing are such wonderful ways to express happiness and joy.

We had one more tradition to complete. We needed to draw names for next year's Christmas gift exchange. My sister-in-law volunteered to cut up scraps of paper for the drawing. "There's no need for that," I said. We called everyone together so I could explain that some of the snowflakes hanging from the ceiling had family member names written on them. Everyone needed to select a snowflake with a name on it, and then purchase a gift for that "flake" next Christmas. The smaller kids looked like kernels of popcorn as they crouched down near the carpet then exploded with a burst of energy to propel themselves toward a targeted snowflake. The adults simply walked around the room harvesting the snowflakes they wanted.   Soon the snowstorm was reduced to a light flurry. Everyone was happy and tired so the migration up the stairs began. But there was one last event to take place, one last memory to make.

While everyone was enjoying dessert, I had snuck to the upper level to complete a very important task. Mother had trained us all very well about keeping our home clean. When we entered the house, we were always expected to remove our shoes, placing them on a clear plastic mat by the door. She felt that by removing our shoes, we didn't track dirt into the house, and it kept the carpet clean. What she didn't realize was that being in our stockings made us feel comfortable and relaxed. My task was to take one shoe from each pair and hide it in the back bedroom. I then took the remaining shoes and created a huge mountain of footwear on the mat by the door. I was in the kitchen doing dishes as each family emerged from the basement with gifts and leftovers in hand, only to discover they couldn't leave because everyone only had one shoe. Of course, because I was in close proximity, I was the first person to be interrogated. After a frantic search of the house, each family found their missing shoes. We all laughed at the prank, and oddly enough no one questioned who had done it.

It wasn't until many years later, that I realized the symbolism of the missing shoes. Initially, I wanted the prank to make everyone laugh before they left the party. But later I realized that one shoe is worthless. You've got to have a pair for them to be useful. It seemed like that was what we needed that first Christmas without Mom and Steve. We needed each other, just like a pair of shoes. We could have each spent Christmas in our homes with our families, but being together, remembering Mom and the Christmases of the past, helped us to heal.

The basement was a symbol as well. We all thought of the basement as cold, dark, and even scary, just as sorrow and loss can be thought of as cold, dark, gloomy, painful, and scary. The basement was transformed to a Christmas wonderland with lights and mementos just as our sorrow had been transformed into a celebration of life by our wonderful memories of Mother, and Christmases of the past. She loved Christmas. She loved us. She helped all of us love Christmas. Now, our Christmas gatherings would include Mother's spirit as well. She would never physically join us for the holiday, but she would always be in our hearts every year when we joined together to celebrate, to laugh, to love, to enjoy, to relish old memories, and create new ones, and to draw strength from each other. Mother would have wanted it that way.

Reflections

•Death is part of the cycle of life. With that in mind, we must realize that we will all experience the loss of a loved one, and we will all experience sorrow. How we express that sorrow is as individual as each person.

•We need to realize that we cannot stay in the state of sorrow. We need to travel down the path of the grieving process to the point where we can celebrate the life of our loved one. Even though we will be changed forever, we need to continue with our own lives.

•There are things we can do to help us move from sorrow (darkness) to light (celebration). We can enjoy photographs, continue traditions, share memories, create symbols and memorials, and have a good cry.

•Just like a pair of shoes, we need to realize that there are times in our lives when we need each other.

Shirley Wegner's Legacy

A Band of
Merry Elves

*"The art of longing and the art of belonging must
be experienced in life."*

-Author Unknown

Have you ever wondered what it would be like to
have your own band of merry elves? There seems
to be a lot of benefits associated with having these
mystical creatures as friends. They are so cute, and
they are always happy. The added bonus is they
can do things for you like make toys, bake
Christmas cookies, and wrap gifts. But let's be
serious for a minute. You can't just place a
classified ad for a band of merry elves.

Fortunately, sometimes what you wish for is
right in front of your face, if you only take the time
to look for it. Such was the case for me. I was
working with a group of students at the reading
table in my third grade classroom, when I looked up
and surveyed the room. Why hadn't I realized this
before? I lived and worked with a room full of
"elves." Granted most people called them third
graders, but come on, they were the right size.
They were cute. They were happy. They didn't
make toys, bake cookies, or wrap gifts, but they did
sharpen pencils, pick up trash on the playground,
and erase the chalkboard. Yes, I could see it now.
With just a little tweaking, I could have my own
band of merry elves. I couldn't give them pointy
ears or make them wear the wacky curled up shoes,

175

but they could wear hats. Yeah, that was what they needed . . . hats.

That weekend, I headed to the local Walmart to purchase thirty red and white Santa hats. It was the week before winter break, so I decided to give the students their Christmas gifts early. When they walked into the classroom Monday morning, each third grader had a gallon sized Ziploc bag on his or her desk. Inside was a sharpened Christmas pencil, a candy cane, a skip an assignment pass, and a fuzzy Santa hat. Although the gifts were simple, the kids loved them. Everyone immediately put on his or her hat, including me. It took the students a few minutes to decide how they wanted to wear their new fashion accessories. Some kids plopped the hats on their heads, letting the white ball hang down the back of their necks. Others tried the furry ball on the left or right side for a sassy, stylish look. Of course, the class clowns put the ball directly in front of their faces, until they realized that it was distracting and interfered with their vision.

Maybe it was just my imagination, or maybe it was a sluggish Monday morning, but the students seemed so quiet that day. It was about 11 o'clock when I surveyed the room from the reading table. The metal bands on the kids' Christmas pencils glittered in the overhead florescent lights. The curved ends of the red and white striped candy canes protruded from their mouths. We had decided to enjoy the candy as our morning snack. It wasn't nutritious, of course, but once in awhile, you just need to have a little fun. The most impressive sight was the sea of red and white fuzzy hats. I actually did have my own band of merry elves, and that definitely put me in the Christmas spirit.

When it came time to get ready for lunch, the class sent a representative to the front of the room to ask an important question. "Mrs. Pottorff, can we wear our hats in the cafeteria and out at recess?"

I didn't see any harm in granting their request. Their new headgear hadn't distracted them all morning. In fact, I was glad they were so excited about their gifts, and an added bonus was that they were going to keep their heads warm at recess for once. You see, I was a transplant from the Midwest, and I noticed right away that kids in Colorado do not dress warmly in the winter. In fact, they wear shorts all year round. It didn't matter if it was seventy degrees or twenty below zero; shorts were the clothing of choice. I think part of this phenomenon came from the fact that the weather in the state changes so quickly. It might be freezing at the bus stop, but by the time recess rolled around, the sun had come out, and it was fifty or sixty degrees in the middle of winter. Colorado kids did wear coats, but to be quite honest, most of the time their coats were thrown in a pile on the grassy soccer field. Hats and gloves? I think they owned these items, but never brought them to school. How the kids dressed really wasn't a battle I wanted to fight. Besides, I believed it was part of their culture. So when they asked to wear their Santa hats out to recess, I was quite surprised, and I was glad for once they would have their heads covered.

It was fun to see them in the cafeteria. Usually, the kids sat at different tables with their friends from other classes and grade levels, but today they all sat together with their red hats bobbing from nodding their heads in conversations. Later, red hats dotted the playground, and it was clear to see who was in our class.

I wanted the kids to wear their hats all week, so I asked the students to leave the headgear on top of their desks before they left school each afternoon. I was afraid if they took the hats home, they would forget to bring them back. Throughout the week, I noticed a change in the kids. They were so quiet and attentive. Generally, they were a very chatty and social group. They lined up quickly to go places, and walked in silence down the halls. Was it just the spirit of the season? Was it their last ditch effort to get on the "nice list" before Santa arrived, or did it have something to do with the hats? As I asked myself these questions, I began to wonder. So I paid even closer attention to their actions and behaviors.

At mid-week, we had an all-school assembly. The entire student body marched to the gym in an orderly fashion. I must admit our band of merry elves looked mighty fine as they sat on the floor in their designated area. Even the sixth graders were a little jealous. After the assembly presentation, there was a question and answer session. The "elves'" hands shot up at the speed of lightning. Most of the adults and students in the room were impressed with their thought-provoking, relevant questions.

Throughout the week they were proud, confident, and they seemed to gel as a group. They received glowing reports from the teachers in art, music, P.E., library, and the computer lab. There was a sudden outbreak of good deeds. Kids were helping kids and were being extremely thoughtful and polite. Yeah, they were different. It wasn't just my imagination.

On Friday morning, the students bounced into the classroom, donned their Christmas headgear, and started their morning work without prompting from me. It was then that I had an "ah ha" moment. The kids really were a band of merry elves. Their hats were a symbol of belonging to a group. Being an elf meant you were hard working, well behaved, thoughtful, kind, and generous. From that code of honor and ethics, came a sense of pride and confidence. I think we all long to be part of a group, yet we also yearn to maintain our individuality. We long for a sense of belonging. It is part of our human nature that can be attributed to the fact that we are social beings. We belong to groups like the Boy Scouts, Girls Scouts, sports teams, churches, and neighborhoods. We need each other. We help each other. We build relationships. That's how we grow and avoid becoming stagnant.

I didn't intend for the situation to be a social experiment. That was simply a "happy accident," a by-product of my simple wish to have my own band of merry elves. The elves learned so much about themselves as a group and as individuals that Christmas. I learned many lessons about basic human nature. I continued to give Santa hats as Christmas gifts each year. It became a tradition in my classroom. I soon realized that I was giving the students more than a piece of Christmas clothing. I was giving them a sense of belonging, a code of ethics, confidence, and a sense of pride. Having my own band of merry elves had more benefits than I could have ever imagined. Not just for me but for the elves as well.

Reflections
•A longing to belong to a group is basic human nature.
•Even though people long to belong to a group, it is also important to maintain each person's individuality.
•Groups have rules, codes of ethics, and expectations that help the members grow, become confident, and develop a sense of pride.

The Polar Express

When the time is right, I, the Lord, will make it happen. Isaiah 60:22

My husband Greg and I had decided to take our children to the Grand Canyon in order to have a fantastic adventure on the Polar Express train. Since we were both educators, we used our winter break to take this epic trip. Five year old Landon and nine year old Sierra were excited to actually experience the train based on their favorite book and movie, *The Polar Express.* When we asked Greg's mom to join us, it was like icing on the cake.

In order to emulate the children in the book, the standard attire for the younger passengers was flannel pajamas, fuzzy robes, and cozy slippers. Once we boarded the train, Landon and Sierra stuffed their backpacks containing coats, hats, mittens, and copies of the book, under their shared seat. They sat on the edge of the seat, clutching the seat back in front of them as if preparing for a wild and crazy ride. In all honesty, none of us knew what to expect. We had read the book hundreds of times over the years, and had recently seen the movie.

The plot of the story focuses on a young boy who rides a magical holiday train to the North Pole. There he meets Santa and is given the first gift of Christmas, which is a bell from Santa's sleigh. He carefully places the bell in his robe, only to find out later that it has fallen through a hole in his pocket.

On Christmas morning, the boy opens a special package from Santa to find the missing bell. Later, he and his sister discover that only people who believe in Santa can hear the bell ring.

Fortunately, our two children could hear the bell. They still believed in Santa. In fact, they were eagerly gazing around the interior of the train car, hoping to catch a glimpse of Jolly Old Saint Nick, and his sidekicks, the elves.

The whistle blew several times, and the conductor called, "All aboard!" Steam escaped from under the car, fogging the windows and obstructing our view. The train made its initial lurch and started into motion to begin our mystical journey. Still clutching the seat back, Landon and Sierra glanced at each other with wide-eyed anticipation. As the speed of the train increased, the sound of the wheels clacking against the tracks could have easily lulled us to sleep if we weren't so excited. Even the stars in the night sky were twinkling to suggest something magical was about to happen.

The first order of business was to feed the hungry children and their parents. Servers dressed in black pants and white button down shirts offered the passengers warm chocolate chip cookies and cups of steaming hot chocolate.

After indulging in the glorious sugar fest, the waiters and waitresses morphed into dancing, singing entertainers. They jumped, bounced, and pirouetted in the aisle as they sang snappy, upbeat Christmas songs. The passengers happily sang along and clapped to the rhythm of the music. The train car felt as if it was about to burst with Christmas spirit but also a sense of anticipation.

Suddenly, there was a jovial laugh from the back of the car. Instantly, all the singing and dancing stopped. Sierra grabbed the collar of her brother's robe, bringing his face close to hers.

"It's Santa Claus," she whispered. Landon's mouth dropped open in sheer disbelief as he gasped for air. They both kneeled on the seat in order to get a long awaited glimpse of Saint Nick at the back of the train car. Santa's entourage included several adult sized elves who walked in the aisle in front of him handing out candy canes to the stunned yet excited children. Santa followed, taking the time to exchange a few words with each child. In the process, he handed each young person an object. From where we were seated in the middle of the car, we couldn't see what the object was.

Finally, Jolly Old Saint Nicholas was standing in the space directly in front of Landon and Sierra. He cordially asked them their names and what they wanted for Christmas. Even though they were mesmerized by his appearance, they managed to find the words to respond to his questions. As he wished them Merry Christmas, he placed a large silver bell about the size of a tangerine in their hands. It was the first gift of Christmas just like in the book.

As I soaked in the astonished looks of our children, I realized it was worth all the time and effort it took to experience this moment as a family. What had just happened was a memory none of us would ever forget.

After Santa exited, the train car was filled with the sound of jingling sleigh bells. Each child on board was eager to try out his or her gift and to test the theory that they could hear the sound of the bell proving they still believed in Santa Claus.

Landon and Sierra retrieved their Polar Express books from their backpacks and were quietly enjoying this timeless piece of Christmas literature. Periodically, they would stop to ring their bells checking to see if they still believed.

It was then that I realized one of the important keys to fully enjoying this experience. It was all about timing. Landon and Sierra were the perfect ages to appreciate the Polar Express extravaganza. Landon was old enough to understand the concepts of the story. Sierra was young enough to still believe in Santa Claus. Greg and I had controlled the timing of this event in order to utilize the experience to its maximum potential.

Our heavenly Father is also in control of the timing in our lives in order to maximize the potential of the events. I thought about the role of timing in many bible stories. There was Noah and the building of the ark. The timing of the Israelites escaping from Egypt and their wandering in the desert for forty years was another examples. The ultimate timing was the birth of Jesus. God's son came to earth in human form right when humanity needed Him the most. Many of the planet's inhabitants were suffering through the reign of the Roman Empire. They felt like they had no hope and were ready to give up, when Jesus arrived in the form of a newborn baby. He offered them hope at a time when they needed it the most.

Just as Landon and Sierra had trusted Greg and I, their parents, to find the perfect time for them to experience this Christmas phenomenon, we must trust our heavenly Father for the perfect timing in our lives. We must trust His decisions. We must trust the plans He has for each of us. Just like the children on the train, we must believe in Him, in his guidance and love. We must believe.

Reflections
•We must trust God with the timing in our lives.
•We must believe in the existence of God. We must believe in His plans for us, and His unending love.

Ornament Envy

Simplicity is the ultimate form of sophistication.
-Leonardo Da Vinci

Have you ever suffered from ornament envy? It is an annual occurrence for me. About a week after Thanksgiving, my family starts begging me to cook something that is not made of leftover turkey. I head to the local Walmart, thinking I can pick up a few groceries and start shopping for Christmas gifts all in the same trip. Big mistake.

Once the automatic glass doors open, and I step inside the massive store, my will power mysteriously disappears. The sound of familiar Christmas songs lure me to the garden department, which has been transformed into a Christmas wonderland stocked with trees, lights, wreaths, ornaments, and inflatable holiday lawn decorations. The twinkling LED lights quickly put me into a hypnotic stupor, and soon I am drawn to the decorated Christmas trees like a moth is drawn to a porch light. I stand for several minutes in front of each tree admiring the elegance and beauty of every ornament. I gaze at the glass bulbs, which reflect the lights and distort the surrounding images. I chuckle at the cleverness of the thematic trees, which include collections of gingerbread cookies and houses, miniature sporting equipment, cartoon animals, snowflakes, stars, or colorful bows. I marvel how everything matches in color or is related to the given theme, which creates an impression of sophistication and class.

While the Walmart garden center at Christmas could suck the logic right out of my brain, the ultimate danger zone was the local shopping mall. Inside those concrete walls there is always a Saint Nick's Christmas Shop and the ultimate haven of holiday ornaments . . . The Hallmark Store. The decorations in these stores are not only aesthetically pleasing, but they touch me on an emotional level as well. There are Santas, elves, snowmen, reindeer, and Christmas fairies, which are so realistic that I expect them to jump into the palm of my hand and carry on a conversation.

"Danger. Warning. Retreat," the logical side of my brain says.

"I must have these beautiful baubles," the irrational gray matter counters.

My solution is to simply leave the shop and vow I will someday have a Christmas tree like the ones in the stores. A Christmas tree decorated with ornaments that matched in color and theme. A classy, sophisticated tree that will be the envy of all my friends.

That is how ornament envy starts each and every year, and if it isn't treated in a timely manner, it can lead to a nasty, itching rash and a migraine headache. What is the antidote for this condition, you might ask? For me, the cure is to go home and decorate our family's Christmas tree.

I couldn't rationalize cutting down an evergreen tree in order to have it adorn my home for a few weeks before throwing it out by the curb for the trash collector to haul away. It seemed like such a waste of a living organism. So, shortly after we were married, I talked my husband into purchasing an artificial tree when they were on sale following the holiday season. We chose one that was seven feet tall, very full and realistic looking. The only things missing were the sap and the smell. With an artificial tree, it is easy for me to embark on my recovery from ornament envy. The tree components are stored in tubs in the basement, just waiting for someone to haul them upstairs for assembly. Usually, my husband does the hauling, and both of us do the assembling. Once the tree is built, my hubby is done with Christmas decorating and leaves the ornament placement up to me.

Ironically, even though I am enamored by Christmas ornaments, I have never purchased one for our family's tree. All of the ornaments we own have been given to us as gifts. The collection began when my sister sent me handmade ornaments when I landed my first teaching job in South Dakota. The PTO members of the first school I taught at, made each teacher a clay Christmas bear that I proudly hung on my tree. That year I experienced what many teachers across the nation experience each holiday season, an outpouring of gifts from the children they teach. I was smothered with homemade cookies and candies, coffee mugs, and gift certificates, and of course, beautiful Christmas ornaments chosen with the utmost care. The ornaments were proudly given, each with the child's name inscribed in permanent marker on the bottom along with the current year. If the name and year were missing, I would add it myself to commemorate the occasion. Over the nearly thirty years I was a teacher, my collection of ornaments grew. Each year when I placed the precious ornaments on the branches of our tree, the symptoms of my ornament envy would dwindle. The itching rash would vanish, and the migraine would fade away. In my imagination, I could see the face of each child who had given me an ornament. I would remember something special about each student, a silly giggle, a persistent attitude, a sense of craftsmanship, a spark of leadership, or a giving spirit. I would begin to wonder how I could long for a tree with ornaments that matched in color and theme? What was I thinking? Our tree did have a theme. The theme was love, plain and simple. Each ornament had been given with love from a sincere student to a grateful teacher. Love. What could possibly be classier or more sophisticated?

Reflections
•Envy is a waste of time and energy. Be grateful for what you've got.
•Keepsakes are physical and can help unleash memories, which are intangible.
•Even though our Christmas tree is simple, it reminds me of a book. Each ornament represents a chapter in my professional or personal life.
•There is no better theme than love.
•Truly, simplicity is the greatest form of sophistication.

The Elf

"The miracle is this, the more we share, the more we have."   -Leonard Nemoy

Living with our son, Landon, makes every day an adventure, but this was especially true during Christmas. While still a preschooler, Landon discovered people had nicknames. After this discovery, he was convinced Santa's real name was Mary Christmas, and Santa Claus was just a nickname. We tried to convince him otherwise, but it was of no use. He wasn't going to change his mind. So Santa was known as Mary Christmas at our house that year.

The year Landon was eight, he really seemed to have the Christmas spirit. As soon as winter break began, and the kids were home from school, Landon decided to wear his fuzzy Santa hat twenty-four hours a day. He bathed with it on. He slept with it on claiming it prevented his hair from getting messed up, and it helped him sleep. The hat had other benefits. It made a great stocking cap when he went sledding and kept his head toasty warm.

Finally, on the morning of the fourth day, I asked Landon to remove the Santa hat, so I could check the condition of his hair. Just as I had thought, he had the worst case of "hat head" I had ever seen. My motherly instincts kicked in, and I quickly lured him into the bathtub with the promise of Transformer bubble bath. I scrubbed his head with baby shampoo as we discussed a new plan of action regarding the hat. The plan allowed Landon to wear the Santa hat each day until Christmas, as long as he removed it each night during bath time, so I could wash his hair.

The following year, Landon had an assignment in school to write about what he wanted for Christmas. When he brought the finished, graded project home, I was very impressed with his wishes. He wanted a new job and a new car for our nephew, Shane, who was living with us. He wanted the rest of us to have good food and to be appreciated more by the people around us. I was surprised he didn't ask for anything for himself. I think that is the true spirit of Christmas, to think of others before yourself.

When Landon was ten, he became the family elf. Two weeks before Christmas, a sign appeared on his bedroom door which read: Elf Factory, Elfs Only! Off Limits! Caution: Many Gifts!

Landon the Elf spent many days in his bedroom with the door closed. Occasionally, he would emerge for tape, wrapping paper, and snacks. I guess even elves need to eat in order to keep up their strength.

One night, I woke up about midnight and saw a light shining from under his bedroom door. Even though I wasn't an elf, I peered inside the room to find Landon hidden under his comforter weaving a potholder for Grandma Inez. I gently reminded him that all elves should be asleep by midnight. He agreed, and put away his loom for the night.

On Christmas Day that year, we were all presented with the gifts from Landon the Elf. I received a small, plastic, Dalmatian puppy and a handmade braided blue and white key chain. His sister Sierra's gift was a deck of snowman shaped playing cards. Grandma Inez marveled at her hand-woven red and yellow potholder. I must admit my husband Greg's gift was the best of all. He received a green Smoky the Bear ruler, a set of pop-up snowman crayons, and the Right Guard deodorant our nephew Shane had left behind after he moved back to Iowa.

It was always important to Landon that Christmas gifts came from him whether he made them or gave away his own possessions or in this case, Shane's possessions. In the end, I think we all learned the best gifts are the ones that come from your heart.

Reflections
•The true spirit of Christmas is thinking of others before yourself. Just as God the Father thought of us when He gave us His son, Jesus, on Christmas.
•The best gifts are the ones, which the giver spends time and effort to think about and create. Those gifts are given from the heart.
•Perhaps it is the giver that is more important than the gift.

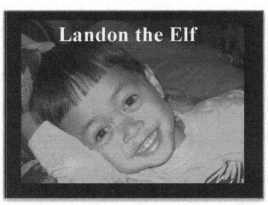
Landon the Elf

The Compass

"Parents can only give good advice or put their children on the right paths, but the final forming of a person's character lies in their own hands.

-Anne Frank

There comes a time in our lives that we all dread. It is the stage in life when we each become "adult orphans." Our parents pass away, and suddenly we become the oldest living generation.

The first Christmas after both of my parents passed away, I felt terribly lost. I lived in Colorado with my husband Greg, young daughter, and son. When we returned to Iowa for the holidays, we always stayed at my parents' home, but not this year. My siblings who all lived nearby, had sold or given away all of Mom and Dad's possessions in an effort to get their house ready to sell. I appreciated all of their hard work, and I felt guilty I hadn't been there to help. Living a few states away had its disadvantages.

My older sister, Barb, who lived in our hometown, had invited us to stay at her home during the holidays. We gratefully accepted her invitation. My siblings had told me I could clean out the garage of my parents' home in an effort to absolve my guilt. It might sound like a monumental task, but it really wasn't. My parents were very organized people. Their garage was probably cleaner than most people's homes.

We all had gathered at Barb's home for Christmas. We did what we usually did. We ate roasted turkey, salads, desserts, and Christmas cookies that Mom usually made. We exchanged gifts in our usual manner.

Now, it was the day after Christmas. The kids were busy playing with the toys they had received. My husband, Greg, was being held captive by the big screen TV in Barb's basement. Barb was out doing errands, so I decided it was an excellent time to walk to Mom and Dad's house across town and begin to work on the garage. It was actually a good day for a walk. There wasn't a cloud in the sky. The air was crisp enough to require a coat, but not cold enough to feel uncomfortable.

The garage door of my parents' home was always unlocked, and today was no exception. I stepped inside and was greeted by an aroma, which was a mixture of dust and motor oil. I found a strange relief in knowing the door to the house was locked. The contents of the house had been sold, and all that was left was an empty shell. The house had always been filled with the love and laughter of family members, friends, and neighbors, but now it was silent and lonely. My parents' truck and car had been sold, so the garage was just as empty as the house.

I walked to the perimeter, grabbed a box and hauled it to the center of the room. I spied a folded lawn chair hanging on the south wall. I removed it from the nail it was hanging on, and unfolded it next to the box. I parked myself in the chair and began sorting the contents of the box into two piles. It seemed sad that everything my parents owned, everything in their lives could be sorted into two

194

categories, throw away or keep. That thought seemed to be the key to the gate of emotions that I had been holding back. My grief, my sorrow, my sense of loss, my raw heartbreak came rushing through my being. It was as if every cell in my body felt sadness and pain. I bent over in the chair, held my head in my hands and cried. My sobbing shook my body like an earthquake tremor shakes the earth. I cried until my body had no more tears left, and my stomach hurt from the physical, gut-wrenching sobs.

Enough of this nonsense, I thought to myself. Mom and Dad would not approve of such carrying on, and I wasn't accomplishing anything. I dried my eyes on my coat sleeves, then walked over to Dad's workbench to retrieve a box of trash bags I needed to complete my sorting task. I ran my hand across the collection of hammers, wrenches, and screwdrivers that were neatly hung on a pegboard attached to the wall. My hand finally rested on the tool my Dad used to remove the oil filters from our cars and truck. Dad always changed the oil in his vehicles himself. He even had two metal ramps to drive the cars up to achieve the right angle, and to get under the automobiles with ease.

Suddenly, my sorrow was replaced by memories. I was taken back to my senior year in college. I was scheduled to complete my student teaching at three different Catholic schools. I was going to start the mornings at the middle school, then walk across the street to the elementary midmorning, and spend the afternoons at the high school, which was in a different part of town. Up until this point, I had relied on the city bus as my mode of transportation. Unfortunately, my teaching schedule and the bus schedule did not match. I needed a car. The idea of purchasing my first car was scary and exciting at the same time.

I called Dad and explained my situation. I asked him to pick out a used car for me at a dealership in a nearby town. I told him the price range I was comfortable with, and asked him to cosign a loan at the bank for me. Finally, I gave him a deadline. I would be home to pick up the car in one week.

"No problem," he responded. "I'll get right on it." Nothing was ever a problem for my father. He had an easy-going personality and did whatever needed to be done without complaining.

For the last time, the Greyhound bus carried me home Friday evening. My parents greeted me at the bus stop with hugs and a multitude of questions. The next morning, Dad and I headed to the bank to sign the necessary papers, then we drove to the car dealership. We both greeted the salesman with hearty handshakes. "I'll have the car brought around to the front," the salesman informed us.

My heart was pounding in my chest from the anticipation and excitement, as the gold, two-door Mazda pulled into a parking space at the front of the dealership. It looked perfect as it gleamed in the mid-day sun. It seemed almost too good to be true. The car was the right price. It had low mileage on the odometer and good gas mileage at the pump. It was clean and cute, and I really liked it

The salesman handed me the keys, and I headed to the parking lot anxious to take my new "wheels" for a spin. I carefully opened the door and settled into the driver's seat. *Yep, it was perfect.*

I was surveying the interior when I noticed a slight problem. Suddenly, Dad was tapping on the driver's side window, so I rolled down the glass.

"What's the matter? You don't look very happy," Dad questioned.

"It's a stick, " I responded. I was referring to the fact that the car had a manual transmission, which would have to be put into various gears using a clutch on the floor and a stick shift lever between the seats.

"What's the matter with having a stick?" Dad asked.

"Nothing, except I don't know how to drive a stick," I responded.

Dad had to drive my new car home, and I followed him in his big, blue Chrysler. When we parked in the driveway, Mom came out to meet us.

"Why aren't you driving your new car?" she queried.

I quickly explained the situation. On the drive home, I had done a lot of thinking. I had decided that I would have to learn how to drive the car in the next few days. As we stood in the driveway, I explained my plan to my parents. They agreed that there was no other choice.

We ate lunch, then Dad and I headed out to the gravel roads of rural Iowa for a driving lesson. Fortunately for me, Dad was always kind and patient and this situation was no different.

Unfortunately for Dad, for someone who was studying to be a teacher, I was a very slow learner. I kept popping the clutch out too fast, which killed the engine. I continually ground the gears and could never find reverse. When we returned home, I honestly thought Dad and I were suffering from whiplash caused by having our heads flop forwards and backwards from the jerky way I drove the car.

After supper, Dad informed me that the learning wasn't over yet. What did he mean by that I wondered? We headed for the garage. Dad told me to pop the hood and the lesson began. Seventy-five percent of the human body is liquid. I began to wonder if the same was true of vehicles. Of course, you put gas in cars. There is the motor oil, antifreeze, and wiper fluid. Dad talked me through how to check the levels of all of these liquids. It seemed simple enough. Then Dad looked at me and said, "Now you are going to change a tire."

That did not seem simple to me, but Dad was sitting on the steps to the house ready to talk me through the task. He had been very adamant that I do everything myself. He guided me through the steps of the other maintenance tasks to ensure I knew how to do everything independently. I removed the jack, tire iron, and spare tire from the false floor in the trunk, but after that I had no clue what to do. With Dad's careful step-by-step instructions, I was able to raise the rear driver's side of the car and pry off the hubcap with the tire iron. Everything was going well, until I tried to get the lug nuts off. I just didn't have enough upper body strength. Dad could have easily gotten up from the steps and come over to do it for me. Instead he calmly said, "You're going to have to put your body weight into it. Push on the tire iron with your whole body, not just your arms."

I did, and it worked. The first lug nut loosened, and I was able to take it off. I used the same strategy for the rest of the lug nuts. When the spare tire was finally on, I stepped back away from the car to look at my handiwork with pride and satisfaction. The grin on my face quickly disappeared. I looked at Dad and said, "I'm going to have to take this off and put the real tire back on, aren't I?"

"Yep," he chuckled. "You know what they say, practice makes perfect."

After I put the tire back on and replaced all the tools, Dad and I headed into the house and went to bed.

We went to mass on Sunday morning, then ate a wonderful home cooked meal. I packed my suitcase and threw it in the trunk. Mother had several plastic containers filled with cookies and brownies for me to take back with me. I set them on the passenger's seat with the intention of munching on the goodies during my drive back to my apartment. The last thing I did was to tape a sign that read "Caution, driver learning manual transmission" to the rear window. Motoring around on the flat plains of Iowa had been no problem, but the college campus I attended was at the top of a very large hill. Stop signs on hills were still a bit of a problem for me. When I let out the clutch, the car would roll backwards before I could give it some gas.

Mom and Dad escorted me to the driveway where they each gave me one last hug. I slid into the driver's seat of my first car, ground the gears until I found reverse, then slowly backed into the street. I waved to my parents out of the open window. They waved back as I ground the gears again, until I found first. It was at that moment, I realized how difficult it must be for my parents to let me go. My older siblings had all married at very young ages, but I, on the other hand, was single and independent. I was always off on some adventure, meeting wacky people, learning new things, and exploring the world. Fortunately, my parents always gave me what I needed to face the challenges life had thrown my way. They had given me self-confidence, ingenuity, a sense of right and wrong, faith in God, and lessons on how to drive a "stick."

My memories brought me back to the garage where I finished sorting through the first box. Most of the contents were trash, mainly water damaged Reader's Digest magazines and broken toys, which couldn't be repaired. I looked into the box one last time and noticed a silver circular disc about the size of a fifty-cent piece. I flipped the disc over to reveal that it was a compass. I placed it in the palm of my right hand, and watched the metal arrow point to north. I slowly surveyed the entire garage, almost expecting my parents to appear. In my heart, I knew the compass was a sign from them. There was no doubt about it.

A compass guides you in the right direction. It prevents you from getting lost and if you are lost, it helps you find your way. I had definitely been lost since the passing of my parents. I didn't know where I belonged or who I was. Now it was so clear to me that my parents had given me everything I needed to go on in life. They gave me strength, determination, moral values, faith, a strong work ethic, people skills, and a wonderful sense of humor. Just as Dad had given me the driving lessons and the skills to maintain my first car, my parents had taught me the lessons about life. When I pulled out of the driveway in my first car that Sunday afternoon, they knew I had the skills that I needed to succeed, but it was up to me to finish the learning on my own.

The compass I grasped in my hand was a symbol of everything they had taught me, everything I needed to stay on the right path in life, everything I needed to find my way. Now it was time for me to continue the learning without them. I still have the compass. It is in my bathroom in a basket that holds everything I need to start my day including soap, toothpaste, moisturizer, make-up, and the compass, which reminds me to stay the course and lead a good life. Where will that compass finally lead me? To heaven where my parents will be waiting for me with open arms and accolades of a job well done.

Reflections

•The best way for a parent to help a child is not to do everything for him or her but to guide them, giving them skills that develop their self-confidence and independence.

•In your deepest, darkest hours in life, when you feel lost and alone, don't despair. Your compass, what you need to find your way, is inside of you. You just need to search for it. It is the essence of who you are, how you have been formed by the people in your life, the experiences you've had, and how you have dealt with challenges and have grown.

•Even when our parents pass away, we must remember that they have taught us important lessons that allow us to continue our life journey and to continue learning on our own.

The Nativity Story

"The most courageous act is still to think for yourself."   -Coco Chanel

The barrage of television ads for the latest and greatest toys, Santa showing up at the shopping mall, and the sound of Christmas carols on the radio, always signaled to me that Christmas was near. Each year, I tried to shield my children from the commercialism of the holidays, as well as the myths our society had created to entice families away from the real reason for the season, Christ's birth.

In an effort to make Christmas a little less about Santa and a lot more about Jesus, we began including birthday cake as part of our Christmas dinner. We would light the candles, sing the happy birthday song to Jesus, and enjoy the cake for dessert. The birthday celebration was a step in the right direction when it came to remembering the true meaning of Christmas, yet something more was needed.

Being a person who prefers to process information visually, I began looking at images of the Holy Family in books, at church, on television, and even at the shopping mall. When I took the time to be more observant, what I saw amazed me. I realized that for my entire lifetime, I had accepted the images of Mary, Joseph, and Jesus without question or logic, for that matter. Mary was usually portrayed as a blonde, blue-eyed, beautiful young woman. Joseph was a young man with long, brown hair and a beard. The birth of Jesus was not only a miracle, but so was the physical appearance of this precious baby. He usually had blonde, curly hair, which was surrounded by a strange, glowing, golden orb. Even though He was a newborn baby, He was about the size of a two month old and as active as a child that age.

Up until this point, I hadn't taken the time to logically think about what the Holy Family might have looked like. Mary and Joseph lived in the Middle East. Usually, people living in this region of the world had dark hair and eyes and beautiful tan or olive skin. Mary was a teenager, a mere child herself. Joseph wasn't much older. Jesus was a newborn baby who was bald or had dark, newborn hair. He probably weighed six or seven pounds and was wrapped in cloth, which didn't allow Him to move around. Even though He would grow up to be the Savior of the world, at this point in His life, He was very helpless and dependent upon his parents.

For years, I looked for more realistic images of the Holy Family to share with my children, but I couldn't find any. Finally when the movie *The Nativity Story* came to the theaters in 2006, I thought I had found a realistic portrayal of the story of Christ's birth. The teenaged actress, Keisha Castle-Hughes, played Mary so convincingly, from her initial fear to her ongoing faith in God. The actor, Oscar Issac, showed a wonderful human side of Joseph that is often overlooked. His devotion and deep love for Mary was evident throughout the film. A surprising twist was his fear and uncertainty about parenting a child who was God. The family was completed with the birth of Jesus who actually looked like a helpless, newborn baby.

When the movie came out on DVD, I immediately purchased a copy with the hope we would watch it as a family every Christmas Eve. We gathered in the living room for our first viewing of the movie. Eight-year-old Landon sat on the floor by his Dad's feet, while twelve-year-old Sierra curled up beside me on the couch.

The story progressed quickly and before we knew it, Mary was on her way to live with her cousin Elizabeth. Both women were miraculously pregnant. Mary was pregnant with God's son, and Elizabeth was pregnant, even though she was well beyond childbearing age.

When it came time for Elizabeth to give birth, several midwives from the village gathered around her as she lay on a mattress on the floor. Periodically, Elizabeth would grab the large rope, which was hanging in front of her, in order to raise herself off the mattress. She would scream in pain at the top of her lungs in the process. The first time this happened, I glanced over at Landon to see his eyes were as big as saucers. Still staring at the television screen, he asked, "What is going on?"

My husband, Greg, quickly responded, "Elizabeth is going to have a baby. That baby is going to grow up to be John the Baptist."

"Why does she need a rope?" Landon questioned.

I thought I'd better take this question. "Pulling on the rope helps her push the baby out, and it helps her with the pain."

Landon's reaction mirrored Mary's in the movie. Both swallowed their fear with a big gulp. Landon continued to watch the movie in complete silence. Mary returned to her parents' home, married Joseph, and soon they were traveling to be counted in the Roman census.

After a long journey, Mary and Joseph finally reached the outskirts of the town of Bethlehem. Unfortunately, they couldn't find a place to stay. As Joseph frantically ran through the streets of town knocking on doors, Mary grabbed her abdomen and screamed in pain.

Landon looked at me and exclaimed, "She's gonna need a rope!"

Reflections

•We shouldn't always rely on society to dictate our thoughts or our traditions. I wanted my children to have realistic images of the Holy Family, so I searched until I found them. I wanted my family to have Christmas traditions, which focused on the birth of Christ, so we created those traditions ourselves.

•We must always resist the commercialism of Christmas and continue to focus on the true meaning of the holiday, which is Christ's birth.

•There are times in life when we all need a rope.

The List

"I can bring home the bacon, fry it up in a pan, and never let you forget you're a man, because I'm a woman." These are the words to a television commercial jingle for Enjoli perfume, which was popular in the 1980s. While this was a very catchy tune, which was meant to empower women, I personally think the person who created this ad and anyone associated with it, should have been tracked down and punished severely. This ad and many others, created the insane myth that women can do it all, and if we can't then we are failures.

Through necessity, as the world and society have changed, so have the roles of women. From ancient times, when women were considered nothing more than property, to earning the right to vote and owning property themselves, women have banded together demanding to be equal with men.

As I reflect on my own family, I realize how necessity has dictated the roles of women. My grandmothers did not work outside their homes, but they definitely worked inside their homes, raising children and running their households. This was at a time in history when it was common for farm families to have many children. My maternal grandmother had ten children, and my paternal grandmother actually won a local contest for having the largest family in the area, with fifteen children. Truly, it is not in my realm of thinking to understand how much work raising that many children could be. This was pre WWII, so in addition to child rearing, my grandmothers spent a massive amount of time obtaining food for their families. They grew gigantic gardens, canned or stored vegetables in their root cellars. Chickens provided not only eggs, but also meat for the table. Homegrown beef and pork had to be butchered, cured, dried, or frozen. Everything was made from scratch, and only the basic food staples were purchased from the local grocery store. Items like flour, sugar, baking powder and soda, salt, and spices were store bought, but everything else was made in the home. Bread, cakes, pastries, butter, jams, jellies, puddings, and desserts were all made from scratch. I can't imagine how time consuming this was, but so essential to each farm family's survival.

My parents were married only a matter of weeks when my father, who was in the army, was shipped off to Alaska to protect our northern most borders during WWII. His paychecks were barely enough to support one person, let alone two; therefore it was necessary for my mother to work outside the home, sewing and cleaning for other families.

As WWII continued, the men were called to protect our country. Out of necessity, women were needed to complete jobs men had held in the past. Once the war was over, the men returned, taking back the jobs they had held before the war. But women had a taste of what it was like to work outside of the home, to have a paycheck, and control of their own finances. It was a challenge for many of them to go back to the lives they had lived previously.

Once again, necessity changed the roles for women. Society and economics required families to have two incomes in order to survive. My father returned to the family farm after the war. In order to make a living, he needed to farm a certain number of acres. In the beginning, when farming was still done with horses, he had a hired man who helped him. Once farming became more industrialized with the introduction of tractors, combines, trucks, and other farm equipment, my father could no longer afford the hired man. He needed that money in order to pay for the farm machinery. Even with the new machines, farming was still a multiple person job. Out of necessity, my mother became the hired man. In addition to all of her chores in the house, she drove the tractors, and grain truck. While she worked side by side with her husband outside in the fields, he never returned the favor inside the house. My father never cooked or did any housework because he considered these tasks to be "women's work."

As I watched my mother do both men's and women's work, I thought all this work to be terrible drudgery, almost as if it were a horrible curse to be a woman because you were expected to do twice the work. As a teenager, my solution to this problem was to never get married. This plan worked for several years. I went off to college, became a teacher, held several jobs, and lived in a variety of cities. Then the unthinkable happened. I met a nice, fun-loving, physical education teacher who became my best friend and later my husband. So much for my plan of staying single.

We had been married for a few years when we decided to expand our family by adopting a girl and a boy from the Philippines. I truly love our daughter and son, as any mother does, but I must admit, once they entered the picture, my workload increased exponentially.

Each day began at 5:15 a.m. when I dragged myself out of bed to prepare myself for the upcoming day. Then I had two more people to get ready, my daughter and son. When they were small, I would drop them off at preschool before going to work. When they became old enough, they came to school with me. As a teacher, I would spend each day in a small room with thirty high-energy elementary school children then I would spend the evening with two equally high-energy kids . . . my own.

When we returned home from school each afternoon, the kids would have time to play in their rooms, while I prepared the evening meal. After dinner, I would clean the kitchen before focusing on the children. There was homework to be done and baths to be supervised. Then we would read together, write in gratitude journals, and pray. By 9 p.m., the kids were sound asleep in their beds, and that is when I would begin to grade papers. At 10:30, my husband would wake me from my slumber on the couch. I would remove the students' papers, which blanketed me, climb the stairs, and go to sleep in an actual bed. Morning would arrive sooner than I wanted it to, and the cycle would start all over again.

The weekends weren't any better. In fact, I think they were worse. Saturday was dedicated to doing laundry, menu planning, and housekeeping chores. We were fortunate to live in a beautiful home, but it was beautiful for a reason. I kept it that way with a lot of sweat and elbow grease.

Sunday was anything but a day of rest. We would rise early in order to attend mass. My husband would take the kids home so they could play while I did the grocery shopping. I would return home, put away the groceries, and prepare lunch. I spent the rest of the day grading papers, making lesson plans, and writing the weekly classroom newsletter.

For the first few years of this routine, I kept blaming myself for my exhaustion, thinking I wasn't using my time wisely. Finally, I decided to consult a few of my friends who were working moms. Unfortunately, they were struggling with the same issues. It appeared we all had the same question as to how to balance work, home and family, but none of us had the answer.

As the years progressed, I found myself resenting my husband. His career path led him to become a middle school assistant principal. His job required him to stay after school in order to supervise sport practices, games, plays, concerts, and every after school activity known to man. By the time he came home from work, the kids and I had eaten and finished our nightly routines. On many nights when he finally came home, the kids were asleep in their beds. Over the years I would lament over the fact that as educators, my husband and I spent so much time focusing on other people's children, we often had little time for our own.

Even though we were both educators, and we both worked extremely hard, our jobs were different. While my husband put in extra time at work each day after school, the extra time I put into my job was each evening at home and on the weekends. He didn't have papers to grade, lesson plans to create, or newsletters to write. While I did these tasks on the weekends, he spent his time watching TV in his easy chair.

Some women dream of the fairy tale in which a handsome prince whisks them away to a castle to live happily ever after. My dream was that when I asked my husband, who was sitting in his recliner, to lift his feet to clean the carpet, he would grab the vacuum cleaner from my hands and exclaim, "Let me vacuum the living room for you."

I didn't expect our marriage to be a fairy tale, but I did expect it to be more of a partnership when it came to cleaning, caring for the kids, and managing a household. After all, my husband had been a bachelor for many years before we were married. During those years, he did his own cooking, cleaning, laundry, and grocery shopping, so I knew he had those skills. But the day after our wedding, he suddenly developed selective memory loss, forgetting all of his housekeeping skills. It wasn't until many years later that I realized when I said, "I do" on our wedding day, I was really saying, "I do it all."

A friend of mine once told me if it weren't for women Christmas wouldn't be celebrated. I was beginning to think she was right. Each holiday season, I would decorate the house, send Christmas cards, shop for and wrap the gifts, and do the holiday baking for family and friends.

One year as Christmas drew near, instead of feeling the Christmas spirit, I was feeling overwhelmed. Not only did I have work at school and home to complete, but I also needed to complete the additional Christmas tasks. By this time, several years had passed, and my anger and resentment about managing our home had turned into a monstrous beast. This fact, coupled with my total exhaustion, was a dangerous combination.

It all came to a head one evening when one of the kids couldn't find an item, which was needed for school the next day. I was in the middle of preparing dinner, and I wasn't in the mood for a scavenger hunt. Because I wasn't going to stop what I was doing to find the item, my child decided to have a "melt down." The tantrum was the straw that broke the camel's back. All the years of pent up frustration came pouring out.

I calmly shut off the burners on the stove, retrieved my coat from the front hall closet, and walked out of our home. I had no idea where I was going. All I knew was I needed to get away. Far away. Away from the chores. Away from the responsibilities. Far away from the never ending work, work, WORK!

It was early December, which meant it became dark outside early in the evening. I followed the streetlights and ended up at the neighborhood school playground. I sat down on a hillside under a large evergreen tree, and there I had a good cry.

I found myself longing for the days when I was in my twenties and life was fun and carefree. At that time, I had lived in several large cities and enjoyed the activities a metropolitan area had to offer. I went to concerts, explored museums, enjoyed movies, and attended parties. I did whatever I wanted to do, when I wanted to do it.

Now, I was trapped. How had I gone from a free-spirited, fun-loving, adventure-seeking young woman to someone who was a servant in her own home? *No wait,* I thought to myself. *At least a servant was paid.*

Part of me wanted to go home, get in my car, drive away, and never come back. As my emotions calmed down, I realized I couldn't do that to my family. I loved them too much. Beside that was not a realistic solution. It was just the anger and exhaustion taking over my normally rational thinking. My mind continued to race with other ideas. Perhaps, I could go to a nearby hotel so I could rest. I just wanted to rest, even if it was only for one day. Was that too much to ask? One day of rest was all I wanted, was all I needed.

I was lost. But I had been lost many times in my life, so why was this situation so different? Perhaps, it was because my decision this time would affect more than just me. It would affect my entire family. In the past, when I couldn't find answers here on earth, I would look to the heavens. I would ask God for help, and He was always there for me. I felt this time would be no different.

"Please help me, God. Please show me what to do. Please help me," I pleaded out loud. The answer didn't come right away. There were several minutes of nothingness.

I hadn't grabbed a hat or gloves during my flight from the house. Now, the cold winter air bit my hands, ears, and face. I stuffed my hands into my coat pockets and pulled my collar over my ears. I closed my eyes and waited for an answer.

When the answer came I was surprised it was in my own words. The last sentence I had spoken out loud in my plea to God echoed in my mind.

"Please help me."

I realized just as I had asked God to help me, I needed to ask Greg to help me. I had the answer all along. Just ask. I needed to ask for what I needed.

When I opened my eyes, it was snowing light, fluffy flakes. This was my favorite kind of snow. It was soft, beautiful, and calming. I took it as a gift from God, as a sign. God was telling me I couldn't be out in a snowstorm. It was time to go home.

I rose from my spot under the evergreen tree, and began walking down the street toward our house. As I neared our home, I saw the warm, yellow glow from the windows and the snow beginning to cling to the pine trees in the front yard. I saw Greg and the kids looking out the front picture window anxiously searching for me. It was then I realized there was no other place in the world I wanted to be.

As I walked up the creaky, wooden porch steps, the front door opened, and Greg and the kids greeted me with warm hugs.

"Where were you? We were so worried," Greg exclaimed.

"What is wrong, Momma?" my daughter questioned.

"I am glad you are back," my son added. "Now we can eat dinner."

We all went inside, and I finished cooking the evening meal. As we sat at the dining room table eating, I explained how exhausted and overwhelmed I was feeling. Then I asked the three of them for help. They all agreed they would do whatever they could. When we finished eating, we simply pushed our plates aside. Greg brought a spiral notebook and a pencil to the table in order to write down all the household chores. Once the list was made, we split up the tasks. The kids were old enough to have chores. In fact, they were eager to help and be part of the solution. They agreed to load and empty the dishwasher, and keep their rooms clean. Greg agreed to do the floors, help with the laundry and meal preparation. Even though the majority of the tasks were still assigned to me, I was overjoyed beyond words to have help. I felt as if a massive weight had been taken off of my shoulders.

After a few weeks had passed, I realized we had become a team. On Saturday mornings, the kids cleaned their rooms while Greg and I completed our assigned tasks. The house was clean and ready for the upcoming week by noon. On Sundays after church, we all went to the grocery store together. Greg pushed the cart. The kids would find items on the shopping list. They even did a nice job comparing prices and looking for the best buys. When we returned home, everyone helped to unload the car and put the groceries away. Sharing the household chores had actually brought us closer together.

As Christmas drew near, the entire family decorated the house. The kids took great joy helping me complete the Christmas baking and delivering the goodies to the neighbors. We all shopped for and wrapped the Christmas gifts for the relatives. It was fun for everyone to be an active participant in the holidays rather than having everything done for them. Sharing the holiday tasks had actually put all of us in the Christmas spirit.

Making the list of chores and seeing the household tasks in writing, seemed to be the key to our success. We all realized how much effort it takes to keep a household running smoothly. When I saw other family members' names beside their assigned tasks, I felt relieved. The magical chore list gave me an idea for a Christmas gift for Greg.

Instead of feeling anger and resentment toward Greg, I was feeling gratitude and a whole lot of love. When I asked him for help, he agreed immediately. When the kids saw their dad jumping in to solve a family problem, they wanted to be part of the solution as well.

So I made another list. This one wasn't about the household chores. It was all the things I loved about Greg. When the lengthy document was complete, I rolled it up like a scroll, tied a ribbon around it, and placed it under our Christmas tree. I kept a copy for myself, so the next time I started to feel overwhelmed, I could read it in order to remember how much I love my husband, and to remember all I have to do when I need help is to just ask for it.

Reflections

•I realized that I had set unrealistic expectations for myself. I wasn't perfect. No one is.

•I discovered it is not healthy to work, work, work. Life is a delicate balance of work, rest, and play.

•As women continue to work and build careers outside the home, I believe running the household should become the responsibility of all the family members. Learning to work as a team can draw a family closer together.

•I learned the power of seeing things written down on paper. Seeing is believing. The list of household chores was the key to finding a solution. The list of what I love about Greg was a wonderful accolade for him and a pleasant reminder for me.

•I learned when you need help all you need to do is ask for it.

Pam and Greg

218

Trash Or Treasure

If you change the way you look at things, the things you look at change. — Wayne Byer

One man's trash is another man's treasure could be the ultimate definition of a yard sale, a Goodwill store, or even E-Bay. One year, I found myself with a new teaching teammate who opened my eyes to using this concept in the classroom.

Jill, my new teammate, was also new to our school, but she wasn't new to teaching. I loved this situation because she brought fresh ideas, which were new to me, but ones she had tried and fine-tuned over the years. When she showed me her collection of third grade units, one in particular grabbed my attention. It was an economics unit based on the book *Bunny Money*.

The book focused on two young bunnies, Max and Ruby, who are faced with the challenge of purchasing the perfect birthday gift for their Grandma. The book highlighted how adults and kids make purchasing decisions. The storyline of the book became the foundation of the unit, and the catalyst for creating an economic system in our classrooms.

One of the components of any economy is currency. Fortunately, at the back of the book were two pages of bunny money in the form of one and five dollar bills, along with permission from the author to make unlimited copies of this unique currency. I never thought creating counterfeit money would be part of my teaching career, but that is exactly what happened. Jill and I started cranking out bills in the school's workroom, only these bills had cartoon bunnies on them instead of dead presidents.

Our next step in creating our classroom economies was to make sure every third grader had a classroom job. These jobs ranged from taking lunch count to sharpening pencils, handing out papers to running errands. Our employment program included rotating assignments each week until everyone had the opportunity to experience all of the jobs that were available.

The kids seem to enjoy the classroom economy we were developing, and the weeks seemed to fly by. Fridays were especially exciting because it was payday. Students were called to the reading table one at a time, where I would dole out green one-dollar bills and yellow fives. After I had carefully counted out the bills as payment for services rendered, each student would then hand one dollar back to me to pay their share of the classroom taxes. Then the student's hard-earned money was carefully deposited in his or her wallet, which was a white business envelope.

As a teacher, I found an added benefit to the classroom economy in that I could collect fines from the students as consequences for their poor choices. Talking without raising your hand or forgetting to put your name on a paper, meant bunny money bills would be traveling from the students' wallets into the palms of my hands and back into the classroom coffers.

With money accumulating in their wallets each week, the students needed something to purchase with their cold hard cash. So we began phase two of building an economy . . . entrepreneurship and consumerism. Students were asked to make items, which could be sold to their classmates on market days. As soon as this announcement was made, the classroom began to buzz with conversations regarding product development, marketing strategies, pricing tactics, and let's not forget the classic concept of supply and demand.

But wait. Not so fast. It was time to add another component, delayed gratification. Students could make purchases during the classroom market days, or they could save their money for the Christmas store on the last day of the unit. The magical shop would be filled with items students could buy and give as gifts to their family members, friends, or perhaps their favorite teacher (hint, hint).

Schools barely have money to pay salaries or purchase textbooks, so the question arose as to how to fund the Christmas store. Enter the concept of one man's trash is another man's treasure. In our classroom newsletters, Jill and I put out a call to all parents to donate items they no longer needed. These items would become the inventory for the Christmas store. The response was amazing. Gently used toys and books were perfect gifts for siblings. Neckties and key chains were popular donations intended for Dads. Jewelry, scarves, and kitchen gadgets were just the tip of the iceberg for gifts Moms would enjoy.

A group of moms, who I began referring to as "our elves," canvassed local businesses asking for donations of merchandise that hadn't sold. The elves also purchased items from clearance shelves and bins. These unwanted items from the local businesses (their trash) became our treasure. Thanks to the effort of the elves, the Bunny Money Christmas Store inventory included coloring books, art supplies, notepads, journals, bottles of perfume and lotions, music CDs, hat, scarves, gloves, mittens, wallets, and purses.

As we all know, you never use all of the Christmas wrapping supplies you've purchased. There is always wrapping paper and gift bags waiting to be used next year. Bows left in bags. Ribbon remaining on the rolls; and nametags yearning for names to be written on them. So we sent out a request for families to donate their holiday leftover supplies to the cause. Kids began arriving at school with backpacks bulging with gift bags, wrapping paper, nametags, bows, ribbon, and even cellophane tape. Not only were the backpacks filled with holiday cheer, but so were the smiling faces of the students, as they proudly dumped the contents of their school bags on the reading table each morning. Truly, the spirit of Christmas had grown much like a tiny seed that flourishes into a stunning, flowering plant.

Since the music teacher worked part time, her room was available on Fridays, so I asked her permission to use her room on the Friday before winter break for the store. Of course, she agreed and was happy to play even a small role in our big endeavor.

Once again, I called upon the elves to work their magic to transform the room into the Bunny Money Christmas Store. The elves, my teammate and I worked tirelessly Thursday after school and on Friday before school, so the store could open after lunch. Teaching, lunch and recess duties took all of my time, so I didn't have the opportunity to take a peek at the progress of the store before it actually opened. I simply relied on the skills, effort, and magic of the elves.

Even though the classroom was quiet when we returned from lunch and recess, there was a spark of excitement in the air. The students had their wallets out on their desks in anticipation for their long awaited trip to the Christmas store. We had decided to send students to the store in groups of ten; five students from Jill's class and five students from our class. The five students were to be selected from our classroom "stick box." The stick box was a cardboard container about half the size of a shoebox, which held a wooden craft stick for each student. On each stick was a student's name. We used the stick box on a daily basis to randomly select students to respond to questions during discussions, to show their work on the board, or perform special tasks.

As soon as I read the first five names, those students instantly vaporized from the classroom with their bulging wallets in hand. I took every measure I could think of to insure that the students who remained in the classroom didn't feel like they were being penalized. I had asked the elves to set aside some of our inventory and put it out periodically so the first, last and all the groups in between, had an equal chance at buying quality items.

When the students were in the classroom with me, I tried to create an atmosphere that was fun and light-hearted with holiday learning centers sprinkled throughout the room. There were books to read and enjoy with their friends, an area to create greeting cards, a selection of board and card games to play, holiday puzzles and brain teasers to complete, Christmas crafts to make, and of course, there were cookies to frost, decorate and eat. Whether you were shopping at the Christmas store, or hanging out in the classroom, either location was a mighty fine place to catch the Christmas spirit.

When a student returned to the classroom from the shopping extravaganza, I would draw another name stick from the box, and one more student would skip down the hall to the magical Bunny Money Christmas Store. Upon entering the classroom, the students who had completed their shopping trip would bounce over to the reading table to share with me the tales of their fantastic purchases. Of course, their gifts were wrapped, but they were eager to tell me what each box and bag contained, and about the magical effects these items would have on the people receiving them.

"I can't wait to see the look on my dad's face when he opens this!"

"My mom is going to love this gift!"

"My brother and I are going to have so much fun playing this board game that I bought for him!"

"My baby sister will love this new toy I got for her."

"I bought my Grandma a bracelet. She will be so surprised!"

"I think my Grandpa will like the coffee mug I picked out for him!"

These were just a few of the sentiments that echoed throughout the room. Although the statements were different, the end of each of these conversations was the same.

"Here's a gift for you, Mrs. Pottorff. Open it."

I would carefully take the small wrapped box or gift bag from each student's outstretched hand, and open the gift, which had been carefully selected just for me. I would follow this with a series of interjections expressing my appreciation and gratitude. Then I would ask for a hug, which was probably the best gift of all for both the giver and the receiver.

Approximately half of the students had completed their shopping expeditions when an elf (also known as a parent) appeared at the classroom door.

"Mrs. Pottorff, we want you to come to the music room to experience the Christmas Store yourself. I'll supervise the students in the classroom. You go ahead and enjoy what you have created," she told me.

It felt surreal as I walked through the halls without a line of twenty-seven third graders behind me. Another factor in this mystical feeling was the fact that I didn't know what to expect once I reached the music room. I had helped set up the store on Thursday evening and Friday morning before school, but that was for the foundational efforts like putting out the tables, categorizing the inventory, creating signs, and placing price tags on all the items. Once the bell rang that morning, the rest of the set up was left in the hands of the very capable and very creative parents.

As I neared the door of the Christmas store, I could hear holiday tunes floating through the air creating a calming yet festive atmosphere. Butterflies fluttered in my stomach, as I took a giant step into the doorway. My jaw dropped open in utter shock and amazement as my eyes gazed upon what seemed to be a cross between Santa's Workshop and Macy's Department Store.

Christmas had exploded in the music room. It was so extreme that perhaps holiday crime tape was needed to secure the boundaries. It wasn't a crime that had been committed. It was actually a Christmas miracle that had occurred.

Every nook and corner of the room shimmered and glistened. Twinkling, white lights sparkled from the walls and tables. Silver, red, and green tinsel garland created gorgeous loops on the front of the display tables that outlined the perimeter of the room and created aisles in the center. The tables were covered with holiday wrapping paper as if they were also gifts to be opened. The parents operating the store were easy to spot, not only because of their height differences compared to the students, but also because of their headgear. Santa and elf hats, as well as bunny ears, adorned each happy, bobbing adult head.

The cheerful hum of conversations mixed with the Christmas carols, which were flowing from the room's sound system. Each student had been partnered with an adult elf in order to assist with the shopping endeavor and to assure the experience was a positive one. Partnerships of children and elves, surveyed the contents of the tables, sharing thoughts and ideas regarding gifts suitable for the students' family members and friends. When a purchasing decision was made, the child happily slipped the item into a large, brown, paper shopping bag with handles held by the friendly, helpful elf. Once all the gift selections were complete, the student and elf headed to the checkout table with the overflowing shopping bag in tow. It was there that the exchange of currency for goods was complete.

From the checkout table, the consumer moved on to the wrapping area where he or she could wrap the items or could ask for help from one of the many cheerful, friendly elves. Then the student headed back to the classroom with a bag filled with treasured Christmas gifts and a heart filled with Christmas spirit.

Before I headed back to the classroom, I took the time and the opportunity to canvas the room in order to hug each elf, thanking her for her efforts in creating our Christmas miracle . . . our Christmas Bunny Money Store. It truly was a miracle.

Our little Christmas store reminded me of the real Christmas miracle, which is Christ's birth. Our store had been based on the idea that one man's trash is another man's treasure. The same could be said of Jesus. His mother was a teenager who became pregnant before she was married. His earthly father was a simple carpenter. Basically, his family was poor and lower class. By the societal standards of the time, when He was born, Jesus could have been considered "trash," but from our Christian viewpoint, He was a treasure. He is and always will be the King of Kings, Lord of Lords, Messiah, and Savior. In life, it's not always about the person, the object, or the situation in front of you. It's about your perspective and how you view that person, the object, or situation. Worth doesn't come from outside forces. It comes from inside each of us. It is the importance we assign to what we experience. That is the true definition of value. Because our perspectives and viewpoints are as unique as each individual, one's man trash can truly become another man's treasure.

Reflections

•Christ Jesus was considered to be trash by the society He was born into, but we know He is the ultimate treasure. He is the ultimate gift given to us by God the Father.

•Worth doesn't come from external forces. It comes from within us by the importance we place on people, object, and ideas.

•Perspective is as unique as each individual person, which is why one man's trash can become another man's treasure.

•It's amazing what people can accomplish when they work together. It can be anything from a classroom economy to a real economy to a Bunny Money Christmas Store.

Bunny Money

The Definition
of a Masterpiece

"There are two primary choices in life;
to accept the conditions as they exist,
or accept the responsibility for changing them."
-Denis Waitley

Many times over the years, my husband Greg and I have given our family members an experience rather than a physical gift for Christmas. Christmas 2012 was one of those years.

Our son Landon, our daughter Sierra, and Grandma Inez each received a ticket to the Van Gogh exhibit at the Denver Art Museum. I had carefully boxed and wrapped each person's ticket so that everyone would have something under the tree. On Christmas morning, as the three of them opened their gifts simultaneously, I explained, "Wow, each of you received a box of culture! "

Not only was it a cultural experience but the chance of a lifetime. The exhibit did not include Van Gogh's famous masterpieces such as *Starry Night* or *The Sunflowers*. Instead, it was a collection of pieces, which illustrated how Van Gogh's art evolved over the years of his short life. A Denver businessman had collected many pieces, and also borrowed a few to create the exhibit. Miraculously, the works were only going to be seen at the Denver Art Museum and nowhere else in the world.

Two days after Christmas, we loaded ourselves into the car and drove to the museum. When we saw the sign at the entrance of the parking garage that read the exhibit was a sold out event, we felt fortunate we already had our tickets in advance.

We checked in, obtained our headphones and audio tour, and began our journey into the world of Vincent Van Gogh. The rooms of the exhibit were crowded. It wasn't wall-to-wall people, but we did have to follow along with the ebb and flow of the patrons. Throughout our journey, I would periodically gaze around each room to make sure I knew the location of each family member.

At one point I couldn't see Landon. I remained calm although news stories of child abductions raced through my head. I entered the next room and quickly scanned the area.

Sure enough, there was Landon standing in front of pencil drawings of several nude figures. Of course, where else would I find a thirteen-year-old boy but at the section with nude drawings? As I approached him, I saw a glazed look on his face.

Actually, the human body is miraculous and beautiful, so I didn't want to scold Landon for his viewing choice, but I also wanted him to stay with our family group for safety reasons.

"Let's read about this section and then go find the rest of the family," I calmly told him. I reminded Landon about the importance of staying together in order to be safe. He quickly apologized for wandering off. I could tell he hadn't done it on purpose. He was just so engulfed in the entire exhibit. It was as if he had entered another world.

As Landon and I read about the nude sketches, I had to chuckle. Van Gogh was a self-taught artist, but periodically he would scrape up enough money to take a class or have an art lesson. When a class that drew nudes would meet, the teacher would select the best students to draw the front of the models while the struggling students drew the backs. Van Gogh was considered a less advanced student, so he was continually drawing butts. In the end (pardon the pun), Van Gogh refused to finish a drawing as a form of rebellion against this policy.

Landon and I exchanged thoughts in a great discussion about how awesome it was that a man who started out in the "butt section" of a drawing class, followed his dreams and passion to become one of the greatest artists that ever lived. It was a wonderful lesson in the power of persistence and belief in oneself.

Landon and I were standing at the display, which was in the center of the room. After our discussion, he asked if he could view the pieces on the outer walls before we moved on to find the rest of the family.

"Go ahead," I encouraged him. "Just make sure I can always see you."

As I watched him scurry off, I thought about the events, which had transpired over the last few minutes. When Landon was missing, and I finally found him in the nude sketches display, I could have scolded him for leaving our group. I could have shamed him for looking at drawings of naked people. Instead, I took a moment to calmly decide how I wanted to handle the situation. By explaining my concern for his safety, Landon learned the importance of staying with our group. By reading and talking about the display, Landon learned not to be ashamed of his body. Instead, he learned the naked human body is beautiful and is often considered a work of art. Finally, an example from Van Gogh's life taught Landon about the importance of persistence and self-confidence.

My decisions as a parent were similar to the decisions an artist makes about color, design, and viewpoint. Just as Van Gogh was a self-taught artist, I was a self-taught parent. Both of us worked on works in progress, making changes in our compositions to create the ultimate, perfect masterpiece. Many of Van Gogh's masterpieces ended up in private collections or public museums. As I gazed across the room at my teenaged son who was submerged in a sea of art, I realized he was my work in progress. He was my legacy. He was my masterpiece.

<u>Reflections</u>
•It is important to give experiences as well as physical gifts for Christmas. Those experiences will become treasured memories.
•Just as an artist makes choices about his or her creations, the choices I make as a parent determines the kind of people my children will become. Each parental choice is a brushstroke, which creates a masterpiece.

•Van Gogh's teacher thought the young artist was only worthy of drawing the backside of the models, whereas Van Gogh thought he was worthy of drawing the front sides. His example taught a lesson that it is not important what other people think of you. What you think of yourself is what is truly important. You are what you think you are.

Landon, my Masterpiece

The Lottery

If you want more luck, take more chances.

-Brian Tracy

Living on a teacher's salary made it challenging to give a Christmas gift to each staff member at our school, but I did it anyway. The key was finding items everyone would enjoy that fit within my meager budget.

Often the gifts were homemade by one of Santa's elves, namely me. These treasures included fresh baked cookies, handcrafted bookmarks and tree ornaments. My favorite gifts to give were poems or short stories printed on colorful holiday paper then rolled into scrolls and tied with festive ribbon.

One year, I felt like I had what I considered to be a stroke of genius in terms of staff gifts, scratch off lottery tickets. Let's face it. There is no better way to express Christmas cheer than gambling. When December rolled around, I headed to the neighborhood 7-Eleven to purchase a unique collection of one-dollar lottery tickets. I had never purchased lottery tickets before, so I had no idea what I was doing, but I was willing to take a chance.

As I peered into the plexiglass display case at the checkout counter, I was perplexed and mesmerized by the variety and number of selections. I stood there frozen in time for a few minutes before the man standing behind me broke the spell.

"Hurry up, lady! I haven't got all day," he spewed as he clutched a six-pack of beer and a box of Twinkies. Clearly, he wasn't experiencing the Christmas spirit.

I changed my strategy to focusing on the holiday section of the display case with the hope that narrowing the choices would speed up the process. I quickly noticed there were no scratch off tickets with nativity scenes on them. I guess it was safe to say that gambling and the celebration of Christ's birth weren't a good mix.

"I'll take ten Santas, ten elves, ten reindeer, and eight Christmas trees," I told the young lady behind the counter as I pointed to each of my selections.

"Just tell me the number by each one. I don't care about the designs on them," she instructed me as she snapped her gum and gave me an impatient look. So I did what she told me to do. She reached inside the display case to get my tickets then placed them on the counter. After she growled the total amount due, I handed her my credit card in an effort to leave the store as quickly as possible.

"You can't pay for lottery tickets with a credit card," she informed me as she rolled her eyes. "It has to be a debit card or cash." *How was I supposed to know that? Fine? Where was everyone's Christmas spirit? Note to self. There is no Christmas spirit to be found at the local 7-Eleven.* I paid the grumpy girl, grabbed the lottery tickets from the countertop, and headed back to my car. My next stop was the Dollar Tree Store.

Once I was inside the dollar store, I felt like I was in my element. I took my sweet time selecting the perfect box of glamorous Christmas cards complete with glitter lettering. I proudly placed my one and only purchase on the black, conveyer belt at the checkout area, along with a one-dollar bill and a collection of pennies to cover the tax. There was something about the feeling of satisfaction that one gets with paying for an item with cold, hard cash because that is what you wanted to do and not because you're forced to do it.

That night I sat on the sofa writing a personal message on each card then slipping what I hoped to be a winning lottery ticket inside. When every envelope was complete with a staff member's handwritten name on the outside, I stuffed these wonderful gifts inside my backpack along with the papers I had graded earlier in the evening.

I wondered what it was about gambling that people found so intriguing. Was it the adrenaline rush that comes from that living on the edge feeling? Was it that element of chance when you hope for the positive outcome, knowing there is an equal chance of failure? Ironically, a few scratches from the edge of a coin or a fingernail would decide the outcome of each lottery ticket I had purchased.

The next morning, I arrived at school early as usual. With an extra bounce in my step, I headed to the office. I was excited to deposit my Christmas gifts in everyone's mailboxes. As I cheerfully slid an envelope into each staff member's box, I thought about what I loved the most about that person. One friend had an irresistible laugh. Another was known for her endless generosity. Then there was the colleague with the uncanny sense of humor.

As I deposited the last gifts into the slots, I realized the irony of the situation. I had given each of my coworkers a gift, which was based on pure luck, yet I had found myself to be the luckiest person of all. My gift of gambling with the lottery tickets reminded me of the gamble I had taken when I accepted a teaching job at this school. I had taken a chance, hoping I would fit in, but there was also the chance that this wouldn't be the right place for me. Fortunately, my gamble paid off. Not only did I fit in, but my coworkers quickly became my friends, and eventually morphed into a beloved "family." Not only did I win the friendship lottery, but I had hit the jackpot!

When I took a step back from the wall of mailboxes filled with white envelopes, I realized I wasn't the only winner in this situation. We all were. We had all taken a gamble on coming to this school, and we were all winners. What was our prize? A lifelong, enduring friendship.

Reflections
•Sometimes in life, you have to take a chance and gamble, knowing the outcome maybe positive or negative.

•It's good to periodically take a step back from the chaos of everyday reality in order to realize how lucky you are.

•You don't need a winning lottery ticket to be a winner.

•You can't find Christmas spirit at a 7-Eleven.

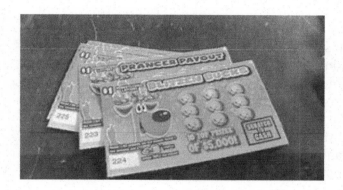

Destination . . . Anywhere

"No matter how bad your situation is, there's always hope if you have faith."

-Author Unknown

I must confess that I love Christmas, every aspect and detail about it. I realize this is true for most people, but in my case I could easily be classified as a Christmas fanatic. I decorate the house before the Thanksgiving leftovers are cold. I buy Christmas gifts throughout the year, stashing them in secret hiding places throughout our home. The piece de resistance of this affliction is that I listen to Christmas music all year long. Because of these behaviors, my son and daughter often refer to me as "weird" to which I reply, "Thank you."

"Why would I want to be like everyone else?" I ask them. To them, this question only adds to my "weirdness."

My husband Greg, our two kids, and I usually rotated spending Christmas in Iowa with my family one year then in western Colorado with Greg's family the next year. This year it was going to be neither of those two destinations. Due to my breast cancer diagnosis in July, surgery in October, and now radiation treatments, we had decided to celebrate a quiet, peaceful Christmas in the comfort of our own home.

I cruised through the holiday season crossing items off of my to do list like a "mad woman." The house was decorated, inside and out. The gifts were purchased, wrapped, and waiting under the Christmas tree. I had made and delivered holiday goodies to all the neighbors. Of course, the Christmas music was blaring throughout our house and in my car.

At this point, the Christmas cards had been delivered. I'd given gifts to my students and the staff at school where I taught. When Christmas morning finally arrived, it was time to exchange gifts with our family. Greg's mom had decided to join us for the holidays. It seemed strange when just the five of us gathered next to the Christmas tree. Usually, we were surrounded by a mob of relatives who created a buzz of happy excitement in the room.

Our son, Landon, and daughter, Sierra, were now twelve and sixteen years old. Anyone who has raised children knows it is a challenge to buy gifts for people who are these ages. They weren't little kids any more, but they weren't adults either. Each time they began to open a gift, Greg and I would tease them a chia pet was lurking inside. Ah, those crazy chia pets, which are pottery shaped like a person or animal. Once water is added, the seeds inside the pottery sprout into plants and become the hair or fur of the person or animal. Much to Landon and Sierra's relief, none of the gift boxes actually contained chia pets. Most contained several articles of clothing and the coveted gifts cards from Amazon and I-tunes.

Finally, one lonely, small package was left under the branches of the tree. Greg picked it up and handed it to me. With a mischievous look on his face, he said, "This one is for you."

"You know how much I love surprises," I said as I began to rip off the wrapping paper. When the paper finally dropped to the floor, I was left holding what appeared to be a DVD case. Strangely enough, there wasn't a title on the cover, only a photo of a man and woman sitting on the grass of what seemed to be the lawn of a college campus.

"What is this?" I asked.

"I'm taking you on a trip!" Greg proudly exclaimed.

"To where?" I further questioned.

"To any where in the world you want to go. I've planned it for this summer when we both have a break from school. I got the DVD from the travel agency I've been working with in town. It showcases the most popular destinations in the world," he explained.

"We're going on a trip!" Sierra screamed with excitement, and soon Landon chimed in with her.

"No, no, no. You two aren't going on a trip. Mom and I are going on a trip. You two are going to Grandma's house," Greg calmly told the kids.

The "We're Going on a Trip" chant came to an abrupt halt. There was a moment of hesitation as the words Greg spoke sank in for all of us in the room. Sierra and Landon briefly looked at each other before beginning to chant, "We're going to Grandma's house. We're going to Grandma's house." Soon they were asking Grandma about all the activities she might let them do that they weren't allowed to do at home.

"Grandma, will you let us drink coffee?" Landon asked. "Can we have ice cream sundaes every night?" Then he dramatically licked his lips.

"Grandma, will you let me drive your car? I can be your chauffeur" Sierra offered.

"What do you think?" Greg asked me above the hum of the kids' conversation.

I do enjoy surprises, especially if I am the person surprising someone else, but there is a distinct difference between being surprised and being shocked. I was definitely the latter. Two people who are public school teachers cannot go on a trip to anywhere in the world.

I was thinking, *what in the world is he thinking?!?!* But I said, "I love it." I hugged his neck tightly and kissed his cheek.

It was a quiet, peaceful Christmas Day. We consumed a turkey dinner with all of the fixings at about 2 p.m. Landon proclaimed it "linner," a combination of lunch and dinner. We grazed on leftovers the remainder of the afternoon and into the evening. At about 8 p.m. Greg, his mom, and the kids had settled in for a night of watching TV. I excused myself to the master bedroom, stating I wanted to read the book Greg's mom had given me as a Christmas gift, but I really just wanted time to think.

I sat on the edge of the bed with the new book in my lap, even though I had no intention of reading it at that moment in time. An image of the travel DVD Greg had given me flashed in my mind. Why had he given me a trip? Had my recent cancer diagnosis made him think I was going to die, and we would never have the chance to travel like we had always dreamed of?

Greg was no stranger to cancer. His father had died of brain cancer long before I met Greg. He knew about the process; the surgeries, the chemotherapy, radiation, and medications. Even though his father went through all of the recommended treatments, cancer still took his life while his son watched helplessly.

Greg's Christmas gift made me question myself. Had I been so busy taking care of other people that I had overlooked caring for my husband and children? I had made the people in the school community where I worked feel comfortable. I had kept them informed throughout the entire process, and I continually assured them that their needs would be met. But had I done the same for my own family?

I have often said that the cancer journey is unique for each cancer patient. But the journey is also unique for each person who has a relationship with a cancer patient.

Landon's way of dealing with my cancer diagnosis was total denial. He didn't want to talk about it. End of story. As far as he was concerned, the only thing that had changed in life was that he rode the bus home every afternoon instead of riding with me so I could have my daily radiation treatments.

Sierra, on the other hand, dealt with the situation with unbridled anger, which was directed at me. I wasn't sure if the cause of her emotions was my cancer diagnosis or the fact that she was a sixteen-year-old girl. Maybe it was a little of both.

I tried to look back to when I was sixteen in order to understand her feelings. At that age, I also had a parent who was a cancer patient, my dad. He had a cancerous lung removed. I don't remember feeling angry. I remember feeling afraid that I would no longer have him in my life. Ironically, even though I was the child and he was the parent, I bustled about him like a mother hen. I reminded him to wear his mask when he went out into the cold, winter air. I suggested he keep a bandana in his pocket to use when he forgot his mask. Finally, when his patience wore thin, he lovingly told me to "lay off."

As I continued to struggle with understanding the reactions of my children and husband, I began to think of the cause of all this turmoil . . .cancer. When you battle cancer, it is imperative to understand the many weapons your opponent has in its arsenal. Cancer is not only elusive but also ambiguous. Even though the word cancer is a noun, you can't really see it or touch it, but you know it's there. It reaches its sinister tentacles into every aspect of your life, your physical being, your financial stability, your relationships, your emotional well-being, and even your spirituality. I wanted so desperately to be able to reach out and grab cancer by the throat in order to choke the very life out of it. Maybe that's how my family felt as well. How can you fight something you can't see or touch? That's when the proverbial light bulb went off inside my head. If we were battling something that couldn't be seen or touched, maybe our weapons needed to be things that couldn't be seen or touched.

I thought Landon and Sierra both needed time. Perhaps with time, Landon would be able to talk and share his feelings with me once we returned to our afternoon car pool situation with just the two of us traveling the rural roads to school and home. Perhaps with time, Sierra would emerge from her cocoon spun with anger and irritation as the beautiful butterfly I hoped she would become. Yes, time would be one of the weapons I would use against cancer, but you can't fight a battle with just one weapon. Love. Love could be my other weapon. You can't see or touch love, but we all know that you can't live without it. It is as essential as the invisible air we breathe. Love and time, these would be my weapons of choice.

By now my thoughts had come full circle, back to Greg and his magnificent Christmas gift.

Perhaps, he had given me two more weapons to add to my arsenal . . . hope and faith. I was stuck in the realm of day to day living; go to work, have a radiation treatment, cook, clean, sleep, repeat. Greg's gift reminded me to look into the future because that is where hope lives; without hope we have nothing. Everyone deserves to dream, to look to the future and visualize what we think it will be like. Dreams and hope are what motivate us to keep going in search of what we think will be a better life, in search of happiness. These ideas seemed somewhat simplistic, but this was my truth. How would we pay for this trip to anywhere in the world? Well, that is where the faith part came into play. We would trust that God would provide. Hope and faith were now two new weapons I had to battle against cancer. How clever of Greg to disguise hope and faith in a travel DVD. At least a DVD was easier to wrap.

I rose from the edge of the bed, made my way downstairs, snuck up behind the couch where Greg was sitting. I planted a big, wet kiss on the bald spot on the top of his head. Then I wrapped my arms around his neck, brushing my cheek against his. "I love the Christmas gift you gave me," I whispered into his ear, and this time I meant it.

Reflections

- Sometimes we become so caught up in meeting the needs of others that we forget to meet the needs of our family members or even our own needs.
- Don't get so caught up in the mundane tasks of every day life that you forget to hope, dream, and think about the future.

- There are times in life when you need to put worry aside and just put your faith in God. He will provide.

Landon, Pam, and Sierra

The White Elephant Gift Exchange

"A good laugh heals a lot of hurt."

-Madeleine L'Engle

Ah, the Christmas tradition of the white elephant gift exchange. There is nothing else like it during the holiday season. I rarely remember the gifts, but I always remember the laughter.

My husband, Greg, actually introduced me to this phenomenon. He was a middle school physical education teacher at the time. We had been dating for several months when he cordially invited me to his staff Christmas party.

"After dinner we always have a white elephant gift exchange," he explained.

"What is that?" I asked out of curiosity.

"You bring junk you don't want and exchange it for junk someone else doesn't want," he clarified for me.

"Sounds interesting," I said as I pondered his eloquent yet accurate definition of the event.

"Each of us will need to bring a gift, but don't worry. I've got you covered," he said proudly.

The night of the party, Greg picked me up at my apartment. Even though the event was casual, we had both dressed up and were looking mighty fine. After a nice meal and a few cocktails, the gift (and I use that term loosely) exchange began.

Beautifully wrapped boxes of various sizes were piled on a table in the center of the room. Each of

249

us had been given a number on a slip of paper when we entered the gathering. The master of ceremonies, also known as the school secretary, excitedly called out the numbers in consecutive order. The person with number one selected a gift from the mountain of packages. After unwrapping the gift, the participant proudly held up the treasure for all of the partygoers to see. Everyone "ewed and ahhed" or made comical remarks about the gift.

There was also another reason for displaying the unwrapped treasure. The person with the next number now had a choice. He or she could select something from the pile of gifts, or he or she could "steal" the person's gift that had just been opened. Now, the plot had thickened. There was one final rule, which was once a gift had been stolen three times, it had found a permanent home, and could no longer be taken.

Soon my number was called. I decided to select a gift from the shrinking pile. Since it was my first time meeting most of these people, I thought I should be nice and not steal from them. Besides no one had a gift worth stealing. I ripped the wrapping paper off a rectangular shaped object to find the movie *Big* starring Tom Hanks.

Greg leaned over and whispered in my ear, "That was obviously brought by a person who doesn't know how to play the game. It's way too nice. Put it in your purse and maybe no one will remember that you have it." Since he was the veteran at this activity, and I was the rookie, I followed his instructions.

He was right. We did go home with the movie as well as a shot of positive energy to Greg's pride with the gifts he had brought to the exchange. The previous year he had scored the coveted frozen fruitcake. The thing was legendary and almost like a school mascot. This delicacy, much like a groundhog on Groundhog's Day, only made an appearance once a year. Every year it would arrive at the Christmas party cleverly disguised in various sized boxes wrapped in festive paper, only to be opened then returned fully wrapped in aluminum foil to someone's freezer until next year.

Greg had retrieved it from his freezer, threw the brick shaped bread into an extremely large box, and covered it with Christmas wrapping paper. An unsuspecting staff member opened it, then held it high as if it were a sports trophy. When I looked at Greg, he was smiling in total satisfaction.

I considered my first white elephant gift exchange a total success. Greg had kept the tradition of the Christmas fruitcake alive for one more year, and I managed to go home with a gift that was actually fun.

Greg and I were married the following year, and I had taken a new job at a rural elementary school. When Christmas rolled around, the school secretary pulled me aside to explain the staff Christmas party traditions. First, the party was always potluck and usually held at a staff member's home. *Great!* I was a good cook, and I could handle that. Second, there was always a white elephant gift exchange. *Sweet!* I thought to myself. *This is going to be fun!*

Greg and I eventually had the white elephant gift exchange down to a science. Many times we would rewrap the gifts we had received at his Christmas party and take them to my staff celebration. Over the years, we saw several wacky gifts including glow in the dark underwear, cassette tapes and CDs of unknown recording artists, movies with obscure titles, neckties that would light up and play songs, ugly artwork, broken toys, and the always popular rolls of toilet paper with jokes or comics printed on the squares.

My school had a particularly outstanding Christmas party one year. A staff member had taken a part time job maintaining an empty house for a real estate company. The house was near her home and had sat empty for several years. Weekly, she would dust and clean the home, and check to make sure everything was in working order. The home had been staged so it was completely furnished. I drove by the house every day on my way to and from work, and I knew it was beautiful. Many of us in the area felt it didn't sell because it was priced at several million dollars.

The staff member/caretaker came up with the idea of having our Christmas party in the empty home. When she asked our social committee what we thought of the idea, we told her it wouldn't hurt to ask the realtor. She did, and much to our surprise, the owner of the real estate company gave us permission to use the home, stating that the house needed some life in it.

The evening of the Christmas party arrived. Staff members trickled in dressed to the hilt carrying crockpots, casserole dishes, and beautifully wrapped white elephant gifts. The evening began with a tour of the home, which was clearly much larger than our entire elementary school. We were awestruck by the gorgeous artwork, furniture, and furnishings. I think each of us suffered from the Cinderella Complex that evening. We were transported from the fireplace cinders to a majestic castle.

After a delicious meal and several rounds of cocktails, we headed to the great room for the white elephant gift exchange. The fun was about to begin.

As always, the gift exchange started out with a bang with the unveiling of an ugly Christmas sweater and a few broken knickknacks. Before I knew it, it was my turn to select a gift. I chose a gift from the pile rather than steal one. No sooner had I unwrapped it, when someone stole it from me. I reluctantly headed back to the gift pile to select another treasure. I opened it, and held it up for everyone to see. Then BAM! It was stolen. On my third trip to the stack of gifts I was starting to become suspicious. I quickly unwrapped a darling but broken pink, plastic, convertible Barbie car. It was perfect for Barbie and Ken to cruise around their neighborhood, but not exactly my size. Immediately, I held it up for all to see, and seconds later my friend, Melissa snatched it from my hands. My suspicions were correct. Melissa is the sweetest person on the face of this planet. She was so sweet that I swear molasses ran through her veins and arteries. It was very uncharacteristic for her to steal a gift at the white elephant exchange. Besides, she had no use for a Barbie car. Her kids were grown, and she didn't have grandkids yet.

"Okay, the joke is over," I announced. Everyone in the room busted out laughing. Knowing how much I love practical jokes, they had all conspired against me. No matter what gift I chose, the next person would steal it from me. The gig was up, so I headed back to the gift pile one last time with the guarantee that no one would steal my treasure. I hoped it would be something good. Much to my surprise, it was a nice gift. I unwrapped a two-tiered serving dish. The two plates looked like peppermint candies, and a cute snowman head adorned the top as a handle. Ironically, Melissa had brought it. She always brought the good stuff.

I, on the other hand, had brought a gift which was either going to be the hit of the party or a total bomb that would be seen as tacky and in poor taste. But hey, this was a white elephant gift exchange. The gifts were supposed to be tacky and in poor taste. That's the whole purpose of the event. That's what makes you laugh. In the end, I was willing to take a chance, willing to live on the edge, and willing to be judged by my peers.

The stack of gifts had dwindled, and the gift exchange was almost over, but my present had not been selected yet. Finally, our new reading teacher chose it. This was a problem. Since she was new, I didn't know her very well. I didn't know if she would find humor in my gift or if she would be insulted by it. As she ripped off the wrapping paper, I sat on the edge of my seat, crossed my fingers, and hoped for a positive result. I glanced across the room to see her holding a gallon sized Ziploc bag on her lap. She carefully read the label. Suddenly, her face turned bright red with embarrassment and her mouth dropped open in disbelief. *Oh no,* I thought to myself. *I am in big trouble.* Much to my surprise and relief, she broke out in a fit of uncontrollable laughter.

"What is it?" several people asked.

"It's a bag of the superintendent's belly button lint," she explained as she held up the bag for everyone to see. There was a moment of silence before the room exploded with laughter.

Unfortunately, at this time we had a young superintendent who had spent the majority of her life pursuing multiple advanced degrees and a limited amount of time actually teaching in a classroom. It was obvious from her actions and demeanor that she considered herself to be royalty, and the district employees were the serfs. She clearly treated others as if they were mere numbers in a statistical equation rather than as human beings with lives, feelings, emotions, and families. To make matters worse, she took every opportunity to insult veteran staff members. She was subtle and always politically correct, yet words like antiques, dinosaurs and archaic would often slip into her vocabulary when referring to older educators. Needless to say, our relationship with her was strained, so I thought perhaps a little humor would sweeten an otherwise bitter situation. I had strategically saved a month's worth of dryer lint, stuffed it in a Ziploc bag, added the label, and "ta dah," instant white elephant gift.

Although the belly button lint was one of my favorite gifts, I had one more trick up my sleeve that I was saving for my last white elephant gift exchange. Just a few short years later, our illustrious superintendent, along with the school board, found a way to rid the district of the antiques and dinosaurs. They announced it would be the last year for veteran teachers to receive severance pay as part of the retirement package. Severance pay had been a tool to keep experienced teachers and to reward them for their years of service in the district. Now, instead of being used as a positive tool, it was being used as a weapon against us. Suddenly, hundreds of district employees filed for retirement. It wasn't just the money, although that seemed to be the straw that broke the camel's back. It was the blatant disregard and disrespect for veteran employees. When you reach a certain age, you expect to be treated with respect. Perhaps you earn it. Perhaps you demand it, or perhaps it is a little of both. No matter. When you no longer have that respect, you search for it elsewhere. Unfortunately, the people most affected by this situation were the students. What most people who aren't in education don't realize is that the staff of a school needs to be balanced between rookie and veteran teachers. Young teachers offer new ideas they have just learned in college. Experienced teachers are mentors for new teachers. They show them what works and what doesn't. Simply put, old teachers teach young teachers all the tricks of the trade and the rules of survival in the classroom that you never learn in college. It's like a recipe in that there needs to be a balance of ingredients . . . young and old, new and experienced, rookie and veteran.

Our little, rural elementary school with approximately three hundred students was heavily impacted by this situation. Eight veteran staff members were retiring, and I was one of them. As the holidays drew near, departing staff members realized this would be our last Christmas party together. When the evening of the Christmas party finally arrived, there was a strange, dark cloud over the usually happy, cheerful event. Eileen, one of the retirees, volunteered to host the party at her home. Her husband, Gale, had spent days preparing the delicious main course. As we did every year, the rest of us arrived with delightful appetizers, salads, side dishes, and desserts. The variety of food reminded us of the beauty and necessity of diversity.

I must admit that teachers, no matter how young or old, are fabulous cooks. Once again, we dined on exquisite, delicious food combined with a hearty helping of friendly, loving conversation.

After a quick clean up in the dining room, we all migrated to the comfy chairs and sofas in the living room. As I glanced around the room, I felt a hole in my heart thinking about the fact that I would no longer work side by side with these wonderful people. They were not only my coworkers, but also my mentors, friends, and soulmates. We were a family who loved and cared about each other. I knew I would stay in touch with them, but it wouldn't be the same as our daily interactions. I thought about the seven other staff members who were retiring with me. Each one was intelligent, fun-loving, kind, generous, caring, and thoughtful. Over the years, several of them had been recognized, won awards, and clearly had won the hearts of the students and parents in our community. This was a group of women who were certainly at the top of their game professionally, yet forced to retire simply because of their age. I truly felt honored and blessed to be able to retire with this group of strong, confident, fantastic women. Even though it was unspoken, I knew many of the staff members were feeling the same way I was . . . nostalgic and a little sad that our days of glory were ending. I was hoping the gift exchange would add the levity that we so desperately needed. As always the wacky white elephant gifts didn't disappoint. It was just what the doctor ordered, which was a healthy dose of humor and laughter.

There were the usual gifts including figurines with funny quotes about teachers, socks with toes, and a hat and purse made of sheared beer cans croqueted together. We laughed as each gift was opened and held up for display.

Finally, the moment I had been waiting for arrived. Eileen, our hostess, headed toward the gift pile and selected the present I had brought. I watched with baited breath as she ripped off the wrapping paper, removed the lid of the shoebox, and glanced inside. She peered inside the box, but showed no emotion. It was as if she was frozen in time. I wasn't sure if she thought the gift was cute, funny, or just plain unbelievable. Eileen carefully reached inside the box and held the contents in her hand for everyone to see . . . a white elephant. It was a toy I had found on the Internet. I simply added a coat of white spray paint to achieve the desired color.

"I love it," Eileen screamed with delight as she rushed across the room to hug me. Eileen and her husband Gale had hosted the staff Christmas party for several years so it seemed fitting and appropriate that she ended up with the symbolic albino pachyderm.

"Please don't steal it from me," Eileen pleaded with her guests. "I really want to keep it." We all agreed she could keep it. The elephant had found a permanent home.

We continued to open our silly gifts and laugh together. Yes, the dark cloud over the celebration had lifted. Somehow knowing that for eight of us, this would be our last staff Christmas party, our last white elephant gift exchange, made us take the first step in the process of change. While we had spent many happy years together, it was time for us to move on. Time for younger staff members to take over the leadership roles we had held for so long. Time for us to seek new challenges and pursue dreams we had put on hold in order to develop our careers in education and to help develop the minds and lives of hundreds of students throughout the years. It was time for us to think about ourselves for once.

As the party broke up, and we each walked to our cars in the snowy driveway, I realized once again the magic of the white elephant gift exchange. It wasn't about the gifts. It was about traditions and inside jokes. It was about camaraderie and being together. It was about creating memories and sharing moments. It was about the healing power of laughter.

Years after that memorable last Christmas party, I reflected on the eight of us who retired that year. Several of the ladies took low stress jobs they enjoyed and loved. Many spent time with their elderly parents and precious grandchildren. Some traveled and others pursued activities they had always enjoyed but never had time to fully experience. Me . . . well, I became a writer. Who would have thought?

We all moved on, changed, morphed ourselves into better human beings, and the added bonus was that each of us was definitely happier. As I reflected on the positive outcomes from a negative situation, I thought perhaps I needed to thank that young superintendent who forced all of us out of our comfort zones. Perhaps a hand written thank you note was in order along with . . . a Ziploc bag of her belly button lint.

Reflections
•Laughter has a healing power. Humor can sweeten even bitter situations.
•Sometimes you need to give up what is old and the familiar in order to move on to what is new and exciting.

A Picture Perfect Christmas

"You will never know the true value of a moment until it becomes a memory."

-Author Unknown

My hand seemed a bit shaky as I nervously moved the computer mouse to drag the family photo folder from the desktop onto the icon for the small external drive. This was the culmination of two years of tedious work, scanning photos from my parents' albums.

The bar across the screen slowly filled with color indicating how many items had been copied. A familiar chime alerted me to the fact that the transfer was complete. I glanced at the bottom of the screen. It read 5,082 items. *Are you kidding me?* I thought to myself. I had no idea there were that many items. Items was a good word to describe what was contained on the external drive. There were more than just photos, although that was the bulk of what I had scanned. There were also documents like marriage and birth certificates. There was the cover of a ration book from WWII, the telegraph my father sent telling his wife that he was coming home from WWII, and I had even scanned his dog tags. There were sweet love letters my parents had exchanged while my dad was in the army.

I glanced at the black external drive protruding from the back of my computer. I felt a sense of wonder and amazement wash over me as I realized my family's history and really a slice of American history was held in a small device which was about two inches long.

I carefully ejected the external drive and inserted another. It was my plan to create a drive of family memorabilia for each of my siblings and my nephew who was like a brother to me. The drives were going to be their Christmas gifts. I was unsure about their reactions to such a gift. Would they just brush it off as one of my many wacky yet creative endeavors? Would they take the time to open the files to look at the contents? Would they find the same joy and satisfaction I had found by delving into our family's history? Bottom line . . . would they be grateful or nonchalant? Only time would tell.

Fast forward to the Sunday before Christmas. It was the family Christmas gathering with my siblings, nephews, and nieces. The attendees of our annual Christmas get together had grown in number over the years. It was difficult to find a place to accommodate all of our family members so we began to gather at my niece and her husband's garage. We felt if Mary and Joseph could have a baby in a barn, then our family could certainly have our Christmas celebration in a garage. It seemed to go along with the "make the most of what you have" theme.

Even though my parents had passed away many years ago, their presence permeated the room. Although no one had suggested it, we had each created one of Mom's special foods to bring to the potluck meal. There was a crock-pot of her homemade hot dish with hamburger, sweet corn, potatoes, and juicy canned tomatoes from someone's garden. There were cocktail wieners dripping with zesty barbeque sauce, dill pickles wrapped in cream cheese and ham, every kind of Christmas cookie imaginable, and to top it all off, warm apple strudel drizzled with powdered sugar frosting.

The buzz of several conversations filled the garage along with plenty of heartfelt laugher. That was Dad's presence. We all had inherited his cheerful, friendly disposition along with his delightful sense of humor.

The endearing chatter continued as we dined on our delicious potluck food. Once the meal was over and the tables had been cleared, the gifts for the name drawing began to be disbursed.

When this task was complete, I asked the "elves" to continue to hand out additional gifts . . . my gifts. The moment of truth had arrived.

Inside each carefully wrapped package was a Ziploc bag filled with childhood photos of each person from Mom and Dad's albums. My siblings and nephew, Robb, also would receive a computer drive containing all the scanned photos. Each gift was adorned with an envelope containing a letter from me. I could hear the envelopes being ripped from the packages followed by the haunting silence as the letters were read.

"I have a feeling this is going to make me cry," someone blurted out, and we all laughed, breaking the uncomfortable silence. This was followed by the rustle and crunch of wrapping paper being ripped.

Then it happened ... a true Christmas miracle. If love could become an action then that is what happened in that room. Each person began with mumbling to his or herself about the memories each photo had aroused. Then the talk spread to the people in close vicinity with statements like, "Look at us in this photo," and questions like, "Do you remember this?" People were moving around the room with photos grasped firmly yet lovingly in their hands, sharing fond memories with anyone who would listen. Even if those photos were sprinkled with fairy dust, they couldn't have been more magical.

As I watched my family interact so deeply and honestly, and I recognized the look of sincere happiness on their faces, I felt a surge of elation and gratitude pulse through my being. This was the greatest Christmas gift I had been given in many years. It was a gift that couldn't be purchased, wrapped or even touched, but it was real ... very real. It was the gift of seeing my family members interact with each other with love and true happiness.

Thanks Mom and Dad, the little voice in my head whispered. *Thanks for giving us photos, for the memories they inspire, and for the love that filled this drafty garage. But most importantly, thank you for giving us each other. Thank you for making us a family. Merry Christmas.*

Reflections

- Photos are often the keys to many priceless memories.
- Usually the best gifts we can give one another aren't things, but the time we spend together, and the memories we create.
- It is important to periodically reflect on the legacy our parents have left us in the form of priceless gifts. These gifts can be an inherited, wacky sense of humor, a collection of family recipes, holiday traditions, treasured memories, or our beloved family members.

Christmas in the garage

Light and Darkness

"I will love the light for it shows me the way,
yet I will endure the darkness because it shows me
the stars."   -Og Mandino

The beauty of Glenwood Canyon in the majestic state of Colorado has always mystified me. The steep canyon walls created by Mother Nature are intertwined with man-made highways and tunnels. Impressive pine trees and black asphalt cling to the side of the mountain in a balance that is both strong and fragile at the same time. If only man and nature could co-exist in harmony like this everywhere in the world.

My family and I were driving through the canyon on our way to celebrate Christmas with my mother-in-law, who lived on the western slope of Colorado. The peaceful scenery and the clicking of the tires on the highway slowly began to lull me to sleep in the passenger seat of our truck.

As I closed my eyes momentarily, the bright orange glow of the mountain sunlight permeated my closed eyelids. Soon I was hovering on the edge of consciousness and the dreamlike world that leads to sleep. Suddenly, the orange glow was interrupted with darkness as we passed clumps of trees, which blocked the sunlight. As we rounded a curve in the highway, the glow returned. The glow and darkness repeated in erratic intervals as we continued our journey through the canyon.

Even though I was half awake and half asleep, my mind was making a connection between this light and dark phenomenon and real life. Those moments of glow were times in my life filled with light when God was speaking directly to me, offering me ideas and moments of creativity, and opportunities for love and happiness, if only I would pay attention and reach out to grab them. The darkness symbolized the times in my life filled with sorrow, depression, and pain.

The intermittent pattern of light and darkness continued as we journeyed through the canyon, just as the intermittent pattern of highs and lows continued on my life's journey. I realized at any moment I could open my eyes and arouse from my pre-slumber to see nothing but light and beauty. Just as in life, I could open my heart and my mind to realize that God is always in my presence, watching over me, providing light in the form of love and guidance through the challenges. Even in the tough times, when life seemed demanding, stressful, chaotic, and events were dismal and heartbreaking, God was always there. Just as the statuesque pine trees and the monumental canyon walls hid the sun, God was always there during the challenges of life even though I couldn't see Him.

Entering Glenwood Canyon is like entering a magical, mystical world. The stone vertical walls rise from the earth, extending into the sky with strength and ease. Giant evergreen trees miraculously cling to the rock walls somehow finding nutrients and water in order to survive. In the fall, the leaves of the aspen and scrub oak trees transform from dark green to fiery red, yellow, and orange. The Colorado River meanders through the canyon floor like a snake slithering through a garden. During the summer, rafts full of adventurous tourists bounce over the rapids and gracefully float in the still waters of the river. Fabricated tunnels and cantilevered sections of highway add functionality to the canyon while maintaining the natural splendor. While the canyon walls block the sun and create a semi-dark environment, there is a beauty and grandeur, which cannot be denied.

The darkness of the canyon had reminded me of the tough spots in life, yet just like the canyon there was beauty to be found in life's challenges. I thought about the dark years when my husband and I were dealing with infertility. We entered the canyon, otherwise known as the adoption process. We filled out paperwork, completed interviews with social workers, took parenting classes, and traveled to a third world country, while the yearning for children to complete our family grew in strength and stature. Through the darkness, we had learned to appreciate the beauty of the canyon. The adoption process had morphed us into different people. We were more patient, mellow, loving, and conscious of the gifts we had been given. We felt God's light when we held our children for the first time. Because of all we had been through, there was a sense of gratitude, which could not be described with mere words. Our journey through the darkness had changed us and led us to the light, our son and daughter, waiting at the portal to parenthood.

I thought about all the times I had to say my final goodbyes to the people I loved including my parents, my nephew, my brother, and my sister. I thought about traveling through the canyon of grief, sorrow, and depression. But I also thought about the beauty within that canyon. The journey had taught me to appreciate the people in my life at a new level. No one was to be taken for granted. Hard topics needed to be discussed. The words "I love you" needed to be spoken and spoken often with sincerity and passion. I learned to see the goodness in people and the gifts they had been given. Most important, I learned to value the parts people played in the puzzle of my life and how their lives transformed me as a person. With God's help, I became a better person. God was the light at the end of the tunnel.

I thought about being diagnosed with cancer. I traveled through the canyon of treatment including surgery, radiation, medications, physical and emotional pain and exhaustion, but I was still able toexperience the beauty of the journey. I learned to see the uncertainty of life as a gift rather than a curse. I learned to live life with greater depth and adventure. Complex matters soon became simple, and the simple matters became cherished. I learned to value time, how to spend it wisely on people and experiences that mattered. The light at the end of the canyon was I became a person who went from merely existing to someone who lived each day of life to the fullest.

Ironically, on that Christmas trip, my physical journey through the Glenwood Canyon led to my spiritual journey in which I learned to appreciate both the light and the darkness. No matter what the darkness in life may be, whether it is financial uncertainty, health challenges, stressful personal relationships, tests of faith, or unfulfilled goals and dreams, there will be a process to complete, a canyon to journey through. I was reminded to see the beauty while in the darkness. There are lessons to be learned there. I was assured there was light at the end of each canyon. With God's help and light, each trial and tribulation in life had made me a better person who had been enriched not only by the light but also by the darkness.

Reflections
•Just as the sun is behind a canyon wall or a towering pine tree, God is always there in our darkest times.
•Beauty can be found in the final outcome (the light), but it can also be found in the process (the darkness).
•Just as we learn to appreciate both light and darkness, we must learn to appreciate not only life's celebrations but the challenges as well.

Glenwood Canyon, Colorado

The Christmas Card Challenge

"Kindness is difficult to give away because it keeps coming back to you."   -Author Unknown

I became an aunt at the ripe old age of three. Crazy, right? Many of my nephews and nieces are about my age and seem more like my brothers and sisters. When they began having children, that's when the real fun began. At that time in my life, I didn't live near any of my family members, so I had to develop creative ways to stay connected to them. I sent birthday cards and gifts, then I expanded the gift giving to Easter, Valentine's Day, Saint Patrick's Day, and of course, Christmas. Cards, letters, and phone calls filled in the gaps between holidays.

As time progressed, technology entered our world, and I was able to communicate with the great nephews and nieces via emails, texts, and even Face Time encounters. Although the use of technology was easy and efficient, I longed for communicating with an old fashioned letter placed in an envelop with a postage stamp in the corner and sent through the U.S. mail. I loved writing letters, and I believed the kids enjoyed receiving them. Seeing their names on a piece of mail that arrived in their mailboxes, made them feel important and grown up.

One Christmas, I decided to take this idea a step further. At the time, I had twelve great nephews and nieces who were under the age of ten. I decided they were the perfect group to experience a simple, social experiment I had dreamed up. I headed to the dollar store to purchase the items I needed to complete this project, which were boxes of fun, playful Christmas cards.

I wrote a letter to each child, asking him or her to participate in Aunt Pam's Christmas Card Challenge. I placed this letter in a large envelope along with three blank Christmas cards. The challenge was to give the cards to people who needed a serving of holiday cheer, an extra dose of love, or a hearty helping of appreciation. Any way we sliced it, we were on a mission to spread Christmas cheer.

I had decided to send each child three blank cards because I felt that was an obtainable number to complete and deliver. I had anticipated that the kids might send a card to each set of grandparents or perhaps one to Mom and one to Dad. After that, the recipients of the cards were in the hands and imaginations of the kids. My goal was to help the children experience the Christmas spirit by thinking about others and their needs. I also wanted them to realize that kindness didn't have to be complicated. Sometimes a kind word or a thoughtful gesture could truly be treasured and possibly even be priceless. I sent the letters and cards off to the designated destinations then sat back to watch the Christmas magic unfold.

My nephews and nieces, the parents of these small children, were happy to help their kids participate in the project. Soon my phone was buzzing with texts, telling me who were the recipients of the cards. One was a neighbor who was sad about the loss of a family pet. Another was a special teacher who went above and beyond to meet the needs of all of her students. Friends from school, a beloved pastor, several Sunday school teachers, and a few favorite cousins received the special Christmas cards that year. One niece decided to expand the project by having her children write Christmas cards for the residents of the local nursing home.

Each time I received a message regarding who had received the cards and how much the great nephews and nieces had enjoyed spreading a little Christmas cheer, I felt the Christmas spirit grow in my heart as well. It's that warm, tingling feeling you get that makes you smile and feel happy. There is nothing else like it.

I was feeling fairly smug about the success of the project, but little did I know that it wasn't over yet. About a week before Christmas, I was sorting the mail. I was feeling a little bummed because as usual, the junk mail pile was larger than the "real" mail pile. Then I came across a treasure. It was an envelope addressed in very distinctive handwriting. A glance at the return address confirmed my hypothesis as to who had sent it. It was from my elementary-aged, great niece, Brynn. My heart rate increased with anticipation as I ripped open the flap of the envelope to find one of the blank Christmas cards I had sent to Brynn, only it was no longer blank. She had filled it with words of gratitude, thanking me for the gifts and letters I had sent to her over the years and voicing her appreciation for my words of encouragement and unconditional love.

A tear slipped out of one eye and landed on the kitchen counter. It was a tear of joy, not sorrow. I quickly found the perfect thank you note in the wooden box on the coffee table in the living room and began writing. I thanked Brynn for the card and pointed out how clever she was to send a card back to me. I shared how proud I was of her for becoming such a thoughtful person. As always, I told her that I loved and missed her. I sealed the envelope, placed a stamp in the corner, and walked it to the mailbox at the end of our driveway.

I know I could have called or sent a text to Brynn, but I wanted her to have something tangible that expressed my sentiments and gratitude, something she could keep, hold, and reread whenever she wanted.

As I walked back to the house from the mailbox, I began to think of the symbolism of the Christmas card Brynn had sent to me. I believe well wishes, positive thoughts, and good deeds come back to us just as the Christmas card I had sent to Brynn came back to me. I had wanted to teach my great nephews and nieces a lesson about giving, but in the end, Brynn was the one who taught me that generosity and thoughtfulness are cyclical in nature. It all comes back to you.

Reflections

•Sometimes you think you are the teacher when actually you are the learner. Perhaps the roles are interchangeable.

•Kindness doesn't have to be complicated. It can be as simple as a good deed, a few spoken words of empathy or gratitude, or several thoughtful words written in a Christmas card.
•Kindness is not only contagious but also cyclical. Eventually, what you give is what you will receive.
•There is great joy to be experienced when you think of others instead of yourself.

Brynn

Snowflakes

"Alone we can do so little; together we can do so much."   -Helen Keller

I have a confession to make . . . I love snow. I love whatever form it takes as it falls from the sky. I love the wet, slushy spring snow that clings to everything, making the world white and clean. I love the dry, grainy snow that drifts across the roads in interesting patterns like desert sand. I love the miniscule snow pellets that look like tiny styrofoam balls bouncing on your windshield as if they were doing a hip hop dance.

Let's not forget all the wonderful things you can do with snow. You can express joy and happiness by dropping to the snow-covered ground and creating a snow angel. You can experience an adrenaline rush by racing down a snowy hillside on a toboggan or sled. You can tap into your competitive side by participating in a good old-fashioned snowball fight. If you're feeling sad and lonely, you can simply create a new friend by building a snowman.

Although I enjoy all kinds of snow and what you can do with it, there is one particular type that is my favorite. It's the fluffy, white precipitation that falls from the heavens like floating balls of cotton. When the flakes land on my clothing, I can see each glorious ice crystal pattern. I always consider each beautiful snowflake a calling card from God, reminding me of His powerful yet gentle nature.

Those snowflakes, those calling cards from God, remind me of God's greatest creation . . . the human race. Just like snowflakes, each person is uniquely different. No two are ever alike. Each snowflake, each person, is a distinctive, extraordinary creation that will never be replicated.

Individual snowflakes have an alluring beauty, yet their delicate, fragile nature is their downfall in that when you touch them, they melt away as if they never existed in the first place. People often have that same characteristic. There are times when people are delicate and fragile even though their individual beauty is maintained. During these times, a cruel act or a few unkind words can cause a person to melt away.

The miraculous thing we must remember about snowflakes is that even though each individual flake is delicate and fragile, when the snowflakes accumulate, they are strong and powerful. Millions of snowflakes create violent, forceful winter storms and blizzards capable of closing roads, shutting down schools, and stopping the ebb and flow of daily life as we know it.

People are like that. One unique, slightly fragile individual can band together with other unique, slightly fragile individuals, to accomplish whatever they can imagine. From women's suffrage to civil rights, the power of people working together is immeasurable.

The next time fluffy snowflakes fall from the heavens to land on your coat sleeve, I challenge you to take the time to wonder at their delicate, fragile, individual beauty. Then ponder on their collective, potential power. See those falling snowflakes as dichotomies, as reminders from God that alone we can accomplish a little, but together we can accomplish so much.

Reflections

•The power of God manifests itself in the beauty of His creations, from the smallest snowflake to the mightiest mountain. We need to take the time to see the beauty around us, and to wonder at God's greatness.

•God works in mysterious ways. He creates dichotomies to challenge our intellect and heighten our sense of wonder. These dichotomies include the delicacy and power of snowflakes and people.

•We, as the human race, must never forget that alone we can accomplish a little, but together, with the help of God, we can accomplish so much.

To think this started as a single snowflake

The Blanket

"The gift is to the giver . . .it comes back to him . . .
it can not fail."   -Walt Whitman

Attending our family Christmas party in
Michelle, my niece, and her husband Chuck's
garage, always reminds me that Christ was born in a
stable. It's not the building that is important as
much as the Christmas magic that happens inside
the walls of the building.

You might ask how our family ended up
celebrating Christmas in a garage. Our family had
simply outgrown everyone's houses. Chuck's
extremely large family had been using the garage
for their family gatherings every Christmas Eve for
several years. Our family decided to follow their
lead by celebrating Christmas in the garage as well.

Many people may think that a garage is an
unusual place to have a Christmas party, but the key
to this scenario was that this wasn't Michelle and
Chuck's first rodeo. Each year, with a little bit of
creativity and an ample amount of elbow grease,
they transformed their garage into a Christmas
wonderland that even Santa and his elves would
envy.

Once the vehicles were removed from the heated
garage, the area was quite spacious and cozy.
Twinkling lights and strings of garland adorned the
walls. A full-sized, decorated tree stood stately in
the corner. My favorite decoration was the sign that
hung by the entrance. It read, "What Happens at the
Christmas Party, Stays at the Christmas Party."

Those words captured the very essence of the garage. We were all safe here. Safe to be ourselves.

When I entered the garage each year, I saw the same familiar sights. The potluck meal complete with all of my mother's signature recipes was located on Chuck's workbench. The men were lounging in the recliners in the corner watching a football game on the big screen TV. Kids were running between the large tables, which had been borrowed from the church across the field. The women were chatting by the beverage station.

On this particular Christmas, everything was the same except for one thing . . . me. I was tingling with excitement because I had a very special gift to give someone. As soon as I entered the garage, I heard her distinct laugh and followed the sound to a table at the far end of the room. There sat my delightful, seven-year-old, great niece, Cecily, affectionately known as Cece to me.

We munched on snacks and appetizers until everyone arrived then the real meal began. We meandered through the buffet filling our paper plates with home cooked delicacies until the plates bowed and bent in protest. When our stomachs were filled to capacity, and the area was cleared of plates and silverware, the designated "elves" began to hand out the gifts from under the tree. Due to the fact that our family was so big, we had resorted to drawing names rather than purchasing a gift for everyone. It was a tradition to hand out the presents to the youngest person first and end with the oldest relative. Finally, the package from me was set before my darling Cece. In an excited flurry of motion, she tore off the ribbon and paper, throwing it over her shoulder to land on the floor behind her. The lid to the box followed in a similar fashion. The moment of truth had arrived. My anticipation heightened. I hoped she would like the gift.

I had miraculously found a company that printed photos on fleece blankets. I had carefully chosen the photos of the various stages of Cece's life. There were also photos of the people who loved her including her parents, grandparents, brother, and in the bottom corner was a special photo of her maternal, great grandmother, who everyone knew as Maga. Maga had recently passed away, and because of Cece's young age, I wasn't sure if she would be able to remember Maga as the years passed. With this in mind, I made sure Cece would be able to see her great grandmother's face and feel her love around her each time she used the blanket.

Jenae, Cece's mom, appeared behind her daughter. As she gazed at the blanket, her eyes focused on the photo of Maga, her grandmother. Tears began to swell in her eyes, but she quickly wiped them away. She grabbed the wrapping paper from the floor searching for the attached nametag to see who had given the gift. She glanced in my direction then walked my way. I rose from my chair because I knew what was coming . . . a big hug. Jenae and I embraced, both crying heartfelt tears. She whispered thank you and that was all that needed to be said. Once we let go, there was my sweet Cece standing before me draped in her new blanket including her head. She reminded me of Little Red Riding Hood.

"Come with me, Aunt Pam," Cece instructed as she grabbed my hand and led me to one of the recliners in the corner of the room. She climbed into my lap and covered us with the new blanket. As the Christmas party continued around us, we snuggled for a few precious moments.

Those few stolen moments were my most treasured Christmas gift that year. The thoughtfulness of a little girl, her willingness to share time with me snuggled in a worn out recliner tucked in the corner of a relative's garage, made all the difference in the world.

The experience reminded me that gifts aren't always fancy, expensive, or even things. Gifts don't need to be boxed, wrapped, or stuffed into a bag. Often, the most treasured gifts are actions that express love. Maybe we are missing that in our society . . . kind actions that express love for one another. In fact, isn't that what Christmas is all about? God the Father's kind act of giving us His Son, Christ Jesus, as an expression of His love for us. Jesus' kind act of giving up His life so all mankind could be saved as an expression of His love for us.

Cece reminded me of the lessons to be learned from the simplistic beauty and absolute genius of the mind of a child. I wanted to give Cece a gift she would always remember and cherish. I wanted her to understand the blanket was a symbol of the love others felt for her. Love that would surround and protect her for her entire life. Love that would last even when someone had passed on to the afterlife. I wanted to give Cece a gift that would eventually become a family heirloom, but what she gave me in return was priceless. She reminded me what Christmas is all about . . . love.

Reflections
•Christmas is about love.
•Because love is abstract, we often need tangible objects, like the blanket, to represent it.
•The mind of a child is absolutely magical. Never underestimate the depth of thinking, the boundless curiosity, the simplistic genius of children. Take every opportunity to learn from them.
•Buildings aren't as important as what happens inside of these structures.
•The love of your family can keep you warm and safe much like the garage and the treasured blanket.
•It doesn't matter where you gather for Christmas, as long as you gather. Spend time during the holidays with the people you care about, create memories, and share the gift of love.
•When you give, you receive a gift as well.

Pam, Cece, and the blanket

It's a
Wonderful Life

*Sometimes things don't work out, not because you
don't deserve it, but because you deserve so much
more.*   -Anonymous

My favorite movie always has been and always
will be *It's a Wonderful Life*. At an early age, I fell
in love with the plotline that all of our lives are
interconnected. As the years progressed, I began to
appreciate another aspect of the movie. I also liked
how the film was based on the reality that our lives
don't always go the way we had planned.

In the movie, George Bailey, played by Jimmy
Stewart, lived a life that didn't go according to his
plan. He continually gave up his dreams to help
others. This eventually led him to thoughts of
suicide one fateful Christmas Eve. These thoughts
led to the appearance of his guardian angel,
Clarence Odbody, who offered the unconventional
intervention of allowing George the opportunity to
see what life would have been like if he had never
existed.

Ironically, the life of George Bailey mirrored the
evolution of the film in that both did not go
according to what was planned. The movie *It's a
Wonderful Life* actually began as a short story titled
"The Greatest Gift" written by Philip Van Dorn
Stern in 1939. After several unsuccessful attempts
to get it published, he decided to self publish the
piece as a twenty-four page Christmas card, which
he sent to two hundred of his closet friends and

relatives in 1943. Clearly, turning his beloved story into a Christmas card was not what Van Dorn Stern had originally planned.

Somehow the Christmas card fell into the hands of actor Carey Grant. Mr. Grant loved the piece of literature so much that he convinced the RKO Motion Picture Studio to purchase it from the author for $10,000 with the hope that he would star in the film version. Unfortunately, by the time the making of the movie was scheduled to begin in the spring of 1946, Carey Grant had already committed to star in another movie titled *The Bishop's Wife*. This was not exactly what Carey had planned, not even close. Enter Jimmy Stewart to play the role of George Bailey. Ironically, this became one of Mr. Stewart's most famous roles, even though he wasn't the first choice for the part.

Shortly after Jimmy Stewart won the Academy Award for best actor in the 1941 film *The Philadelphia Story*, he enlisted in the Army Air Forces. Jimmy, who already had a private pilot's license, wanted to fly combat mission in WW II. The Army officials felt his celebrity status and popularity were more important assets, so he was assigned to make recruitment films and to attend patriotic rallies. Jimmy was persistent with his requests to fly in combat. As a compromise, he was assigned to training younger pilots, and eventually he was deployed to Europe where he spent eighteen months flying B-24 bombers over Germany.

By the end of the war, Jimmy Stewart was one of the most respected and decorated pilots. These accolades came with a price. In 1945 when Jimmy

Stewart returned to the United States, he was suffering from what is now known as PTSD or Post Traumatic Stress Disorder. He had lost a lot of weight and looked very ill. He suffered from nightmares, was depressed, and withdrawn. Due to his condition, many people thought his acting career was over. Then came the role of George Bailey in the movie *It's a Wonderful Life*. The making of the film actually seemed to be therapeutic for Mr. Stewart. In several scenes, George Bailey appears to be unraveling in front of our very eyes as he discovers what the world would have been like if he had never been born. Many movie crewmembers believed that Jimmy Stewart wasn't acting during these disturbing scenes, but was simply allowing his PTSD to be captured on film. In a truly unexpected twist of fate, much like the character George Bailey, whose life was saved in the movie, acting in the film *It's a Wonderful Life* saved Jimmy Stewart's career and life.

As with any film, there were high expectations for the movie, but it was not well received by the public during its premier. It recorded a loss of $525,000 and was considered to be a box office failure. This was not what the movie studio had planned when it first took a chance on purchasing the short story.

Despite being initially shunned by the public, the movie did gain in popularity and was eventually nominated in six Academy Award classifications. Although it was nominated for Best Picture, Best Actor, Best Film, and Best Sound Recording, it didn't win a coveted stature in any of these categories. Ironically, *It's a Wonderful Life* won an Academy Award for Technical Achievement for the development of falling artificial snow, which was a total surprise. Prior to this, painted cornflakes had been used to simulate snowflakes. Director Frank Capra didn't like how the cereal snowflakes crunched under the actors' feet, so he worked with Russell Shearman, the special effects supervisor for the film, to invent an artificial snow from fire extinguisher foam, soap, sugar, and water. Never in their wildest dreams did these two men think their efforts in creating artificial, falling snow would earn them an Academy Award.

You might ask how a story that the author could not get published became a film that lost money during its debut, turned into a Christmas classic that has been voted as one of the best movies of all times? The answer is simple . . . the magic of television. Once the movie reached public domain status, it could be shown without the payment of licensing and royalty fees. In 1976, three decades after its initial release, it became a television staple and a Christmas classic. This unexpected turn of events was a shock to even the film's director, Frank Capra. The unexpected twists and turns in the journey of this film seemed to mirror the unplanned events in the life of the movies' main character, George Bailey.

As I began writing the stories in this book and reflecting on the events in my life, I began to realize the similarities between George Bailey's life and my own. My life certainly hasn't turned out the way I had planned. I never planned on living in the

Rocky Mountains. I never planned on facing the sorrow of infertility or the joy of adoption. I never planned on losing two of my siblings to cancer or facing the dreaded disease myself. Certainly, I never planned on becoming a writer. All of these events were unplanned, but in retrospect I wouldn't have changed a thing. Each high and low, deepened my understanding of life and made me the person I am today. It has been all those unexpected twists and turns that have transformed my existence into what I consider to be a wonderful life.

Sources
•En.wikipedia.org/wiki/It%27s_a_Wonderful_Life
•mentalfloss.com/aricle/60792/25-wonderful-facts-about-its-wonderful-life
•Facebook.com/NedForney

Reflections
•The unexpected events in life are actually blessings, which form and strengthen you.
•Take the time to reflect on the events in your life in order to view them with a sense of wonder and gratitude.
•Never forget that it truly is a wonderful life.

Celebrate Life!

about
The
author

Who is Pam Pottorff?

A child of God, a devoted wife,
Mother of two, lover of life,
A thinker, a dreamer, a rainbow admirer,
A teacher, a student, a cancer survivor,
A think outside of the box type of gal,
A happy soul who wishes everyone well,
One who colors outside of the lines,
An artist, a writer, a friend at all times.
A nature enthusiast, a Colorado resident,
One who appreciates the past, and loves the
present.

Books by Pam Pottorff

Your Christmas Reflections